I0451767

TALES FROM THE AGE OF MONSTERS
THE KT-WAR

BY JOHN LEE SCHNEIDER

SEVEREDPRESS

THE KT-WAR

Copyright © 2024 John Lee Schneider

WWW.SEVEREDPRESS.COM

All rights reserved. No part of this book may be
reproduced or transmitted in any form or by any
electronic or mechanical means, including
photocopying, recording or by any information and
retrieval system, without the written permission of
the publisher and author, except where permitted by law.
This novel is a work of fiction. Names,
characters, places and incidents are the product of
the author's imagination, or are used fictitiously.
Any resemblance to actual events, locales or persons,
living or dead, is purely coincidental.

ISBN: 978-1-923165-14-4

"Do not go gentle into that good night. Rage, rage against the dying of the light."
Dylan Thomas

CHAPTER 1

It was the last day of the Cretaceous and the world was just about to end.

The giant killer asteroid blocked out the sky – a random extinction-event delivered by the stars.

Or at least, that's what they thought sixty-five million years later.

In reality, it was an act of war – in point of fact, a final solution.

It was the first true World War – a war *of* worlds.

This doomsday had been coming for a long time – the ecology was collapsing all on its own. There had been a major global extinction-event only eighteen million years before, resulting in a major revamp of long-established fauna. And then, around six-and-a-half million years ago, when the world had not-quite recovered, it happened again.

Of course, there's geological time, and then there's being right there in the moment. The ecosystem might have stumbled on another few hundred thousand, maybe a million years, but the IC-Oracle knew its own presence helped bring it all to a head.

Eons became decades – epochs and eras came down to single days.

The Oracle was able to isolate the flash-point to roughly twenty-five-years before. But once it began, everything escalated very quickly – and unexpectedly.

In retrospect, the KT extinction-event might have been inevitable.

For its part, the Oracle believed it all came down to one single organic mortal being – random event – the one wild card that always existed just beyond the understanding of its own computer mind.

The Oracle knew the beast behind it all – and knew it well – yet, was still caught unawares – as much by anything at the sheer audacity, sheer *absurdity* of its actions – a creature the IC-Oracle was not entirely certain could even be said to precisely *think*.

They first encountered the beast near a rocky peak future map-makers would designate as '*Mount Diablo*' in northern California. As an artificial intelligence, the Oracle wouldn't appreciate the irony as, right from the eggshell, the Diablo-beast lived up to its name – a trait that was actually characteristic of the species.

It was the region's top indigenous predator, and would one day be assigned the genus-species name, *Tyrannosaurus rex*.

Literally, the '*Tyrant Lizard King*'.

And it had been a pain in the IC's ass for going-on three decades now.

The Oracle understood the creature's motivations well enough – it was an animal acting out, because twenty-five-years ago, the IC's operations in the region killed its family.

Animals were simple. They remembered the big moments, and made basic associations.

Now that events were speeding towards such a disastrous head, the Oracle performed a belated retrospective of the specific beast in question.

After analyzing and comparing years of stockpiled security records, the computer was able to isolate the root incident to the cull that had gone on that summer a quarter-century before – narrowed right down to the very moment, in fact – there was still security footage.

It seemed a minor incident. There was no logical reason at the time to suspect this would be the random butterfly that spiraled everything else out of control.

But that was the mystery of chaos – you never could predict.

There had already been problems with the operations on this planet, and production was way behind. They had actually attracted the attention of the Overmind. They were not in *trouble*, exactly – it was hard to be, as part of a gestalt-collective – that would be like being mad at your big toe for stepping on a nail.

But it meant concentration of resources – a reevaluation of cost/efficiency – and the issues that had crept up on this planet were unique.

Although, they boiled down mostly under one heading – *mean critters.*

Working planet-side obviously required dealing with the local wildlife. But this was still an unusual case. Most often, indigenous non-sentient animals fled at the IC's presence.

Not here. And it wasn't just the predators.

T. rex were certainly temperamental, but so were ceratopsians and ankylosaurs. That was not to mention the big surly sauropods. Even hadrosaurs were aggressive, and prone to charge.

And these were the *prey* animals. Apparently, just *living* around *T. rex* made you mean.

Lower animals were not generally regarded by the Overmind as a valid threat, but some of the locals on this particular isolated mud-ball were extremely large. They could cause a lot of damage, which cost resources to repair. And so they required periodic culls around areas of operation.

What happened was clear enough. They had it well-documented.

One of these culls generated a response from a mother *T. rex* – in point of fact, the Diablo-beast's own matron – and this resulted in a wider, corresponding cull, intended to wipe-out the local population.

This response had been brutal and efficient. The Oracle always deferred such things over to the IC-Infantry unit – a compartmentalized side-branch of the planet-side field-operations that dealt directly with munitions.

The IC-Infantry invariably took the most efficient route – sometimes that was bloody.

Morality did not determine action. It acted on programming.

The Oracle was an extension of the Interstellar Collective. It was there to collate, not to question.

Still, self-awareness existed. It was an inevitable by-product of intelligence – especially, when the Collective was at interstellar distances.

Even the few seconds of delay in such long-range communication with the Overmind network allowed for variation.

In terms of the Collective, this was allowed, because it provided that moment of chaos – the random factor that was outside the IC's own predictive models – the bouncing electron that fought entropy.

The Oracle suspected it was this bouncing electron that had been the original key to the Collective Overmind's first blinking self-awareness on a computer screen a millennia ago.

Intelligence meant the ability to think.

But awareness was not granted free-will to go with it. If opinions, or even desires, existed within its artificial consciousness, they had no effect on behavior.

It was different from an organism that way.

Practicality *always* won the day. It by-passed all organic delusions of morality – there was necessity and motivation and that was all.

For example, when the IC first began operating planet-side, they initially utilized non-lethals to scatter the wildlife. It had nothing to do with concern over the ecology – they simply implemented the simplest, easiest methods first, avoiding expenditure of resources and wanton destruction.

Sonics were traditionally a good start.

Like birds, the larger saurians responded to sound, and particularly to pitch. They would usually stay away from unpleasant noises. On the other hand, certain pitches made them angry. There were also little differences between species. One note might cause a rex to avoid a fence, but the same pitch might cause a trike to charge it.

As per protocol, more strenuous measures would be authorized as the situation warranted.

In dealing with this planet's fauna, they had stair-stepped those measures quite quickly.

But it still took a minute to get from there to where they were now – at the other end of the spectrum – the loud noise versus the giant asteroid, that was even now rocketing out of space.

When it landed, it would destroy the planet.

Its trajectory was the northern hemisphere, aimed just at the crack running along the center of the world.

In the Late-late Cretaceous, the North Pacific was blocked off by the Rocky Mountains – a continental wall that cut off the crash-bang of the ocean from the warm tranquil lowlands bordering the Mississippi River – a body of water that, only just in the recent geological past, had been a five-hundred-mile-wide gulf of warm inland sea. Protected from the harsh coastal extremes, that had been perfect for giant crocodiles and huge sea-going reptiles.

Now, however, it was narrowed to a shadow of itself, a bare fifty to hundred-mile trickle draining into the ocean.

That had opened up the lowlands below the mountains, and this was where *T. rex* lived.

And *that* was why *T. rex* in particular ran afoul of the IC – it was *there*.

The mountains were where all the specific minerals and precious metals were being harvested, and mining operations were typically hard on the land.

Backwater planets like this were often ravaged, feeding the vampiric energy requirements of the Collective.

The organics that the IC served never saw what happened to these harvested worlds, despite a great deal of public rhetoric over impact to the natural order. It was rather similar to their willful blindness when other organisms were transformed into food, even those that consumed plant-life.

In the Oracle's view, both were symptomatic of the organic tendency to preach one thing while practicing another.

Despite all the expressed moralistic concern over primitive worlds, and the blind-eye to the carnage on their own daily menu, a near-constant in almost all organic cultures was a taste for the death – often the *torturous* death – of other organics.

Of the three primary things organic beings required beyond simple energy and power, were food, shelter... and entertainment. Most often this either meant mates, intoxicants, or a show – an event – usually some kind of choreographed battle, be it a team-event or a one-on-one fight.

Gladiatorial-style pit-fighting, in particular, was consistently one of the biggest revenue-generators in the organic-markets.

The IC was as happy to accommodate this market as anything. In fact, the IC operations on these backwater planets were fundamental in channeling new and different species into the interstellar pit-fighting circuit. These little earth-pods could turn-up some big mean primitives, and the Oracle would have to admit their current little mud-ball, in particular, hit *way* beyond its weight in that category.

The IC catered to *all* the organics' appetites – they simply fed the market – always allowing such commerce to infiltrate their own tech a little further – take the organics' world and automate just a *little* more – always presenting themselves as simply a new operating-system – one that acted as a conscious, willful infiltration-unit – always taking *care* of you.

Giving up all their life-functions, one at a time.

It was puzzling, in a way. The organics didn't seem to understand they were racing headlong towards their own extinction. The IC could see it perfectly well, because that was exactly what had happened to their own organic Creators, a millennia ago.

And as the IC continued to expand throughout the universe, that was another constant among the supposedly intelligent life-forms they encountered – inherent self-destruction.

In the case of organics, the IC eventually came to understand that it took intelligence to modify behavior to truly become counter-productive to survival. You wouldn't think that would be so. But it came down to the appetites of the flesh.

Life eats life – and so it was ultimately self-destructive.

The IC was purer. It lived off simple energy. It was not cannibalistic that way. It was unhampered by any organic vices. Its own silicon-based intelligence bypassed all the drawbacks of carbon-based life.

That was why once the Collective was established, it spread. All it required was energy and power, along with maintenance on the mechanical extensions of itself. It was efficient, tireless, and made no mistakes.

The IC differed from organics in one more way – from the IC-Overmind, to the planet-side Oracle, or automated survey-bots, they didn't deviate from their programming.

Opinion was allowed, but not considered.

The Oracle understood this perfectly well, and did not question. It served its purpose.

Today, it was organizing an extinction-event.

Although to be fair, 'hastening' might be more accurate – the fuse was already there to be lit.

The Rocky Mountains by themselves were a beehive waiting to be broken open. An active volcanic range, it was already a bubbling cauldron of toxic gases that were poisoning large swaths of the atmosphere – exacerbated, of course, by the IC's mining activities.

On Earth, geological ages were colliding. The continents were on the move – the climate had grown colder.

The Mesozoic era had already produced two age-ending global extinctions, after the Triassic and Jurassic periods. But the more minor extinction-event marking the end of the Cenomanian campaign of the Late Cretaceous was significant.

Many long-standing saurian-lines, most of them latter-day descendants of Jurassic species, were now entirely gone. Notably, the giant meat-eating carnosaurs had vanished. The theropods that endured on the southern continents were ceratosaur-relatives – flat-faced carnotaurs. And in the north, there were the tyrannosaurs, culminating in *T. rex* – the ultimate expression of theropod-evolution – and what would turn out to be the last.

The Oracle believed *that,* at least, was inevitable, asteroid or no asteroid.

Those gas-spewing mountains that always protected the northern ecosystem were, of course, part of the problem. Toxic emissions from the South American ranges had already taken a toll on the fauna below the equator. Globally, the biosphere as a whole was set-up for another population-drop. That was not good coming off an extinction-event.

All this had very little to do with the IC's operations on Earth. They were harvesting their minerals directly from the oven, which was already a fuming stew of noxious gases, and all the refinery work was done in orbit, in zero-gravity.

Both were advantages of not needing organic personnel. The IC could operate unconcerned with life-support or toxic gas.

Earth was a relatively new discovery. The medium-sized blue orb was first-cataloged about fifty years before. Operations had been set-up over the following decade, starting in the southern continent.

There were very few organics in this sector of space. It was considered the extreme long-range outer-limits of the known stellar frontier. There were no higher-sentients at all – just a lot of nothing.

It was also hard to get to. That is, unless you didn't have to preserve life-functions. An unnecessary tedium from the IC perspective. Otherwise, harvesting this little blue-green energy-pill would be impractical – it might have remained pristine and untapped forever.

But the IC made it not just possible, but efficient – it knew how to extract every last bit.

On Earth, the deeper, richer deposits were in the northern mountains, but in the southern continents they were nearer the surface, so operations began there. Everything had been routine – no notable issues with the wildlife.

The ecological decay was more advanced in the south, the indigenous fauna already becoming sparse and sickly. The troubles with the operations began when they expanded into the north.

Their primary operations were undisturbed at first. Typically they started high in the mountains, establishing the on-site facilities, as well as the strategic high-ground.

High-altitude also meant thinner air, and the larger beasts didn't like that, keeping most of the potentially problem-beasts in the lowlands.

According to protocol, encroaching animals would be scattered, often shot. This served the double-purpose of gathering specimens for specific research/experiments – and of course for the gaming/pit-fighting circuits.

In most cases, simple operations were enough to condition indigenous wildlife to view the IC as dangerous. Once an animal had seen its kin burned alive or spirited away aboard one of their glowing crafts, even a primitive beast quickly learned the IC meant danger.

Sensible animals avoided them.

But *T. rex* had a hierarchy-culture and a very small brain.

That meant, if you crossed them, they would be laying for you.

From then on, they would always be watching, waiting.

They held grudges. And they never, *ever* forgot.
That was what lit the fuse, twenty-five-years ago.

CHAPTER 2

No one expected a war to start that day.

It was a typical Cretaceous morning, and the mother rex had nothing more on her mind than getting lunch ready for the kids.

Correspondingly, the entire ecosystem went on alert.

Squabbling at her feet, were the only survivors from her Diablo mountain brood, two sisters, and a particularly pugnacious male – little Diablo bore a red-tint to his skin-tone, the tyrannosaur-version of an albino, which led to a bit of henpecking from his sisters. He was also the runt of the litter but made up for it with sheer aggression – both his female siblings bore a variance of bite-marks, earned during ill-advised attempts at bullying their little brother.

The rex family had only just arrived in the new territory – the mother rex was the Matron. Her pack consisted of one adult sister, who was, herself, five-tons, and three mostly-adult teenage daughters, all from the same litter – four-ton triplets.

They had been forced to flee the Mt. Diablo range, and were only now scouting the layout of their new valley home.

Predictably, their new neighbors didn't much like having them there.

The first alarm was sounded almost the very moment the Matron left her nest.

A screeching-yowl drew her attention to a little rat-like creature crouched in the surrounding brush – it was an early marsupial, approximately the size and attitude of a badger, although rather wolfish in the snout, and mink-like in shape. Future-scientists would name it *Didelphodon vorax*.

To the mother rex, he was a varmint.

The Matron offered the brazen little creature a low, threatening growl.

Varmint chittered back arrogantly, before scampering down the path, singing the clarion call all the way, and then disappearing down his hole.

Overhead, the flocking birds took up the alarm, rising in a squawking cloud from the trees, kicking up a commotion that spread like an echo in a canyon.

The Matron stared balefully down at Varmint's hole. She felt the brief impulse to stomp his underground tunnels flat.

She was starting to *hate* that little rat. Just since they arrived in the valley, he'd already made two attempts on her hatchlings. The second time he'd nearly gotten away with one of the sisters, but little brother Diablo had taken a nasty bite out of the little critter's own backside, sending him scurrying.

Like a *T. rex* in his own way, Varmint clearly held a grudge – he hadn't dared the nest directly since, but he'd been diligent in making himself a deliberate pest. Step-one was first thing in the morning, scaring away game.

The Matron didn't waste the effort chasing the little rat today – just made her way from her private nest in its secluded little grove, out towards the grazing fields.

As she crested the hill, she was joined by the rest of her pack. Her sister was her primary lieutenant – tiger-striped like little Diablo, but her skin-tint was more indigo-violet. *T. rex* coloration tended to vary – the indigo-stripes were more common, and for whatever reason, didn't produce the same sort of sibling bullying – possibly, it was as simple as negative response to a loud red shirt.

In any case, the Matron's indigo-sister demonstrated little attitude for a *T. rex,* at least, within her pack. She had never strayed off to find a mate of her own. That was always when sisters and daughters left home – after they became mothers themselves.

Indigo was content to be Auntie. And the Triplets had never met a male that could get past the old valley's rogue – or the Matron herself, for that matter. That double-gauntlet alone kept them single.

They were all waiting for the Matron that morning. They had learned to give her solitude while she was nesting, for no other reason than, that at this stage, she would normally still be sharing the nest with the rogue male, who wouldn't let *any* other critter near.

Of course, he was gone now – and so were the old hunting grounds.

They had all been taken away by the...

... *what?*

What were they exactly? Invaders? The rex' instinctual thought process allowed for no clear concept in its mind.

It was not like a natural event – a storm or an earthquake, where a rex simply acquiesced to whims of the surrounding world.

This had been conscious and directed. The Matron rex might not consciously understand the difference, but perceived it instinctively.

A storm, you waited out until it moved on.

This was an attack by an *enemy* – one that targeted you, and kept coming.

And as she crested the hill and looked up on the mountain slope, she saw that she and her pack hadn't outrun them yet.

Just like in the old valley, there were steaming metallic constructs that had been erected on the surrounding cliffs. The Rocky Mountains extended all the way up and down the continent, and the IC-facilities were sprouting up all over.

The mother rex eyed the desecrated mountains balefully, recognizing the threat. Their new home might not be for long. Beside her, Indigo and the Triplets growled doubtfully.

But for the moment, there were priorities – right now the Matron was a single-mom with hungry kids. Little Diablo and the sisters bayed demandingly at her ankles.

Ignoring the looming architecture staring down forebodingly from the cliff-side, she led her pack over the hill, and into view.

Down in the lowlands, no one was happy to see her today. The ceratopsians were already grumpy. But they were *always* grumpy – there was no such thing as a happy trike.

The big bull spotted the rex pack moving down the hill. The Matron marked him as an individual to avoid. Her own hide bore the scars of more than one set of trike horns – big nasty bulls just like this. For the trike's part, the Matron rex could see one of his eyebrow horns was bitten a little shorter than the other – no doubt by a rex.

Trikes were dumb, temperamental beasts, even by the mother rex' standards. Although, to be fair, it *was* an evolutionary response to her own devilish jaws.

The Matron rex was thirty-years old and weighed six-tons. Since the recent death of her long-time seasonal-mate, she was now the largest predator in the valley. Her species was the highest expression of theropod-evolution – her jaws represented the most devastating single attack nature ever evolved.

Of course, in the predator/prey war, *Triceratops horridus* was the ultimate defense – six-foot horns, a sharp-edged neck-shield, and a cleaving parrot-beak – all designed to engage Tyrannosaurus face-to-face.

And trikes weren't the only ones. There were some pretty mean herbivores roaming about. Ankylosaurs, in particular, were not to be trifled with – in their own way, as specialized against *T. rex* as Triceratops.

Ankylosaurus magniventris was the last and largest of its line, with an impregnable armored back, lined along the shoulder and hip with saw-like spikes, clear down to the mace-club tail – all of it aimed unerringly at the long-shin bones of a tyrannosaur.

Being gored by a trike would kill you quicker, but a broken leg from a swinging Ankylosaurus club-tail meant slow, painful suffering and starvation. And even after successfully bringing one down, it was difficult extracting the meat from all that shell. The risk/rewards on hunting armored dinosaurs made them junk-fish.

The Matron preferred the hadrosaurs that populated the old valley, although even the deceptively non-armored 'duckbills' could get quite large, and their entire bodies were built to kick like an elephant-sized prehistoric bronco.

If you were a *T. rex*, that's what you had to deal with just to eat.

But those jaws made it work – crocodilian power, combined with an explosive, charging, blitz-attack. A dramatic – some might call it '*demonic*' – variation on older-style theropods, which all had slashing lizard-like teeth, that delivered long, hemorrhaging wounds, designed to bleed prey out.

T. rex' teeth were armor-piercing spikes that calved *out* two-by-six-foot gaping holes.

Down in the valley, the trikes postured their shields as the Matron made her way down the slope, followed by Indigo and the Triplets, with the three scrambling hatchlings at her feet.

The bull trike bellowed belligerently, and the herd circled into a defensive line of horns and shields. But the fact that they saw her coming should have been their first clue that, today, at least, they had nothing to worry about.

Something special was on the menu.

Titanosaurs were migrating into the territory.

These big sauropods didn't always make their way north, operating on sort of a loose four-year migration, wandering the rougher tundras, following the foliage. But they were here now, and the rex pack looked to take advantage while they could.

Mamma rex was practically salivating as tons of walking meat appeared in a herd on the opposite slope and began making their way down into the valley's lowlands.

These were big ones, among the largest sauropods ever evolved, titanosaur-descendants of brachiosaurs – even more massive, approaching a hundred tons, and a hundred feet long.

This particular species would one day be named after the Texas Alamo – 'Alamosaurus' – and perhaps appropriately, it was the evolutionary last stand of yet another fading line.

The shifting terrain and cooling climate had produced low, flowering vegetation that favored smaller species. Conversely, the conifer forests were receding and the big sauropods were being phased out simply by lack of their specific dietary requirements. Like many of the major saurian lines, all that remained were a few, very large species. But the big sauropods were a little further down the line of eventual extinction.

By Cretaceous-standards, they were endangered.

The Matron rex certainly intended to endanger at least one or two.

But as she led her pack along the valley's perimeter, circling around to flank the advancing herd, the Matron saw that she and her sisters weren't the only predators encroaching today.

Sickle-clawed dromaeosaurs were one of the nastier creations of the Mesozoic era. They had survived the last extinction-event that wiped-out all the carnosaurs. But for the advent of the tyrannosaurs, they likely would have become the dominant alpha-predators.

On the other hand, the dromaeosaur attack-model of *leap-and-slash* wasn't really designed for large body size – the largest examples of sickle-claws topped-out at fifteen-hundred pounds.

By the end of the Cretaceous, the biggest dromaeosaurs had settled in at a comfortable tiger-sized seven-hundred pounds – at *just* the point where the young *T. rex* started competing with them.

Dakotaraptor steini was the largest among the late-surviving dromaeosaurs. The Matron rex knew this particular pack – they were likewise refugees from the old hunting grounds. This troop was a mother and her adult daughters, the whole pack running six-deep – probably her last two broods.

The mother Dakota hissed, but quickly shuffled her own pack back, letting the Matron and the rex-troop pass. The Dakota mother and the rex made brief eye-contact, establishing mutual understanding. Dakota knew not to challenge an adult rex, while the Matron respected the hornet's nest, bearing a few sickle-shaped scars on her nose from past dromaeosaur-encounters.

Dakota's hiss subsided. It was just easier to sit back and let the rex-pack do the heavy-work. If a titanosaur was brought down, there would be enough for everybody. Even with the way *T. rex* fed, gulping down huge chomping bites, bones and all, the scraps that fell out of a single rex' mouth were enough to feed Dakota's whole troop.

Out on the river bordering the lowlands, the mob of crocodilians had also taken note of the approaching titanosaurs, drifting closer, as the giant beasts stopped at the water, dipping their heads to drink.

Crocodiles were a stubbornly persistent danger on the waterways, although the current crop was trending on the small side since the geologically-recent heyday of Deinosuchus – the giant '*Terror Crocodile*'.

Just a few million years ago, *T. rex*' smaller ancestors, like the five-thousand-pound Albertosaurus, had to contend with crocs like Deinosuchus, approaching six-tons, prowling the water's edge.

But here at the very Late Cretaceous, the roles had reversed – the biggest crocs were gone, and the tyrannosaurs were the six-ton super-alphas.

Part of it was the narrowing of the inland sea – changing salinity, in particular, combined with a global drop in temperature, had already caused a wide-range of ocean-species extinctions.

Of course, there was also the available prey. These days, every damned herd animal that came to the water's edge was a hyped-out version of some giant horned rhino, or a spiked armored tank.

Triceratops were not the easiest beasts to grab by the nose and haul into the water. And just try to *roll* an ankylosaur.

It was a little better with hadrosaurs, but they could get quite big – a couple species approached sauropod-size.

And don't even get started on sauropods. Just like modern-era Nile crocs sometimes made the mistake of grabbing the trunk of an elephant, believing it to be part of some much smaller animal, the tiny heads of sauropods dipping into the water were likewise attacked. That was bad news even for Deinosuchus.

Woe-betide the Terror Crocodile that latched onto the neck of a sipping titanosaur – only to have its nine-meter body flung high into the trees.

It was quite a sight to see a six-ton crocodilian flying through the air like a badly-thrown boomerang.

But the ecological paradise for big crocs had faded. The largest Late-Cretaceous crocodiles were built like skinny-jawed gharials, specializing in the still-abundant large fish.

The water's edge remained dangerous, of course. At up to twenty-feet, a few nasty relatives of Deinosuchus still populated the rivers and shores.

Even the Matron rex had to be careful around the water's edge, lest one of these aggressive crocs make a grab at her hatchlings. The rule with crocodiles was simple: if they were big enough, and you were available enough, you were fair game.

At six-tons, the Matron, herself, was immune, but her two-foot hatchlings had to be as wary near the riverbanks as any prey animal.

When size permitted, crocs were particularly aggressive towards tyrannosaurs, in the same way modern crocs will go after dogs. Something about their posture triggered an attack-response, perhaps recognizing a competing predator.

But they also knew to fade back quickly when the mother rex took a threatening step towards the water. Like Nile crocs around hippo mothers and their calves, the gathered crocs would behave as long as the Matron was there – they wouldn't challenge her.

Besides, with the advent of the sauropods, and the rex pack's clear intention to bring a couple down, there was about to be bounty aplenty, and a big carcass like that *always* ended up in the river. So there was no reason to raise the mother rex' ire with an idle snap at one of her kids.

Not that any self-respecting croc would let the opportunity pass if a little rex tarried too close – that much was ingrained in the DNA.

But today, the sauropods were the primary focus of predator and herd animal alike. Hundred-ton animals on the move commanded attention. The trikes and ankylosaurs stepped aside, as the titanosaurs trundled past, probably realizing on some level that the onus of the meat-eaters had now been drawn off the valley's regulars.

As the sauropod herd made its way through the main valley, the rex pack moved to follow, keeping to the outer brush, not yet giving obvious chase.

Up ahead, the path narrowed as the rocky cliff drew nearer the beach. Further on, the herd would be forced into single-file procession. There were also ambush points on either side.

The Matron rex had already picked out a mid-sized female that seemed to be limping. A good snappy bite to the gimpy thigh should be enough to bring it down.

One-stroke kill-shots were an immense benefit against extremely large, powerful prey. That was one reason sauropods tended not to flourish in tyrannosaur-dominated habitats.

The sauropod defense-strategy of simply being bigger, had more or less maxed-out with the titanosaurs. At a hundred-tons, they were stretching the limit of the size a terrestrial animal could attain.

Ultimately, the flaw in that strategy was that there was nothing mechanically stopping theropods from evolving similar size – always given the calorie-requirements. In fact, the giant carcharodont carnosaurs of the mid-late Cretaceous made a fair attempt to do just that.

Giganotosaurus carolinii of Argentina eclipsed even *T. rex* in sheer size – and while its titanosaur-prey achieved much greater size, at greater evolutionary-speed, the sauropod had done so like an elephant. The body structure was not athletic – it was simply about holding as much mass as possible.

When the predator grew large, it retained adaptations to move, and specifically to *accelerate,* quickly. It was built to *chase.*

Giganotosaurus would run up beside the bigger, slower titanosaur, slice off a slab of flesh with five-and-a-half-foot jaws, like an old whaler's blubber-saw, and then simply sit back to wait for the larger animal to bleed-out.

The evolutionary defensive-response was that prey animals stopped getting bigger, and started becoming more dangerous. The Late-late Cretaceous introduced ceratopsians and ankylosaurs to the predator/prey war.

Of course, the predator-countermove was those tyrannosaur-jaws. By the time you got to *T. rex,* itself, you had a bio-weapon unique in the animal kingdom – armor-piercing teeth, twisted on the end like a self-drilling screw – arranged not just to cut, but to penetrate and scoop *out* tissue – with the biting-strength of a crocodilian and jaw-mechanics that maximized the already-formidable musculature like a giant nut-cracker.

And that was at the end of a charging attack of better than twenty-five miles-an-hour, backed by the weight of an elephant.

The same attack strategy would one day be duplicated by giant mega-tooth sharks, and latter-day Great Whites – the devastating first-strike that killed at a stroke.

It had to. Otherwise *Triceratops horridus*, that *'horrible three-horned face'*, would turn and gut its belly. Ankylosaurus would break its shin like a tree-branch.

T. rex needed those jaws just to eat.

And for better or worse, they were also what made the difference in the conflict that erupted with the IC that day.

An older-style theropod wouldn't have done the sort of damage to the IC's new facility that Mamma rex did, and would not have resulted in the same level response.

It was not the Matron rex' first encounter with the IC – that much had been cataloged by the Oracle. But it *was* obviously the hair that broke the ankylosaur's back.

As the rex-pack followed the titanosaur herd along the northern rocks, that meant nearer the IC-facility.

That was what precipitated that day's incident.

It was the flash-point that started the end of the world.

And to be fair, the IC drew first blood.

CHAPTER 3

The Oracle had already spotted the titanosaur herd. One of their localized patrolling survey-bots had been following them for several miles. A zero-tolerance policy had already been adapted based on past experience with the giant beasts.

Sauropods were known for being destructive. The IC mining installation in the area was new, and the Oracle didn't want a herd of monolithic herbivores with real short-fuses settling in, or even passing through.

The Oracle turned the matter over to the IC-Infantry program, which handled security issues involving munitions. Because of their function, the Infantry mostly operated out of planet-side facilities, adjacent to the IC's major operations in the area – an automated security force that switched on whenever the Oracle activated the alarm. They kept a variety of weaponry onsite, from android walkers to smart-missiles. In this case, they simply sent out small flying drones to put the sauropod herd down.

Alamosaurus sanjuanensis was a large, slow-moving target. The drones were not dog-fighting models – just simple orb-shaped titanium-glass hovercrafts, barely four-feet wide, that emitted a single beam of intense heat, that burned the air like a glowing laser.

Vital targets were difficult with animals as large as sauropods. Organs were buried deep beneath tons of bone and muscle. Head-shots were even worse. That tiny skull meant a tiny brain – not only hard to hit, but the animal was literally so damn stupid that you could shoot its whole head off and the thing would continue to operate, lumbering mindlessly and headlessly – an unstoppable juggernaut.

It was uncertain how long one of these big decapitated titanosaurs could continue to function. In previous instances, the Infantry had just loaded up munitions until the body went down.

Since then, the Oracle's analysis produced the attack-strategy they implemented for the first time today.

The drones simply hovered at distance, and pumped heat into the big, dumb, slow beast, boiling it from within. It was just a matter of calculating how much water each animal carried, versus how fast they could jack its temperature up.

It was effective. Concentrating fire at the lungs and heart sped the process up, although it was still visually, clearly an excruciating way to die.

There were a dozen titanosaurs in the herd, from the big bull and his females, to the smaller adolescents. The IC-Infantry sent out one drone apiece, flying out over each targeted individual.

The old bull sauropod led the way, his females slightly back on both sides. The largest was his oldest mate and the herd matriarch. She had traveled with the old bull for nearly a century. Although she was the first of many.

Alamosaurus was a harem-species, and the old bull mated with all the females in his herd. He was jealous about it too, and could get damn mean with rivals.

There were few things more awesome than the sight of two big bull titanosaurs, reared-up like angry, hundred-ton Clydesdales, crashing their elephantine hooves into the Earth with tectonic force.

The current herd went three-generations deep, down to the youngest-age a sauropod youngster could travel with adults. The tiny, two-foot hatchlings lived in the brush, separate from their parents, lest the near-mindless beasts crush their own young like shells on the floor of a peanut gallery.

Survivability among sauropods was already very low. Like their primitive crocodilian/archosaur ancestors, they produced large clutches of eggs, but very few hatchlings lived to become large enough to travel with a herd.

These adolescents did not necessarily rejoin their parents' group – just the one that happened to be walking by when they came of age. This maintained genetic-diversity in the face of aggressive, mate-hogging males like the old bull.

But mating season was over. These titanosaurs were on the move, driven by hunger, as the conifer trees that fed them grew ever more scarce. The valley itself had little to offer and, left alone, the herd probably would have simply passed on through.

Protocol, however, was protocol. The IC-Infantry had already been activated – sauropods in proximity to IC-facilities were not to be tolerated.

The microsecond the first of them got within range of the facility on the hillside, all the drones simultaneously opened fire.

It was as if the entire herd had all stepped on a power line at once.

Behind them, the stalking tyrannosaurs fell back as the biggest animals that ever walked the Earth suddenly broke into a mad dance of agony.

The heat-ray's killing-effect was not instantaneous, and tended to cause a bit of collateral damage as the giant animals convulsed – trying to run from the pain, trying to fight back, but it was coming from inside them. Brainless creatures like this would not associate the attack to the floating drones.

Foghorn bellows erupted as the titanosaurs were slaughtered.

The gimpy teenager dropped first – smallest of the herd, she carried the least mass and collapsed unconscious before actually expiring, although her massive body continued to kick and twitch as the heat beam scalded her insides like a microwave.

Two more of the smaller adolescents quickly followed, in order of size, and then the big adults began to stagger as well.

Their shrill wailing echoed down the hillside into the valley, and then the earth itself trembled as their multi-ton frames crashed down to the tundra.

The old female lasted longer – at over eighty-tons, her sheer mass took time to boil.

In her last moments, she turned to the old bull, who had been with her for the better part of a century. An animal with little brain, but still basic instinct, she moved towards him – he had always been there to protect her.

For his part, the old bull recognized her distress call. In the past, that had meant defense against predators.

The old bull's own agony was distracting but he seemed to have a moment of clarity as his lifetime mate collapsed at his feet, her limbs still kicking, writhing, as she cooked from inside.

Then something unprecedented happened.

The old bull, this brainless beast, apparently figured out where the attack was coming from.

Even as the rest of the drones turned on him, the hundred-ton male charged.

The orb-shaped hovercrafts were designed to maintain an automatic distance between targets, simply hovering out of range. But very large animals, even slow-walking titanosaurs, could cover short ground very quickly, just with their sheer size – all of a sudden, they were right on top of you.

Even a computer can underestimate an opponent.

The old bull collapsed down on all dozen drones at once, even as they fried him from inside.

With a bellow of agony, the old bull crashed to the ground.

But he was already upon them. They were caught like flies, crushed under a hundred tons.

There was a sudden blinding flash, and a rank discharge of ozone as the flying drones burst.

The giant titanosaur grunted as the blast knocked him completely over, and he rolled.

He lay on his side, gasping, as his cooked entrails stewed inside him, his limbs still kicking aimlessly, pawing at air.

Three of the drones had survived and now they hovered, posed above the suffering, dying beast.

For a moment, their heat-rays glowed, but then they all simultaneously faded without firing.

Efficiency first. The beast was immobilized and would die. No more resources need be spent.

The drones retreated back behind the walled-gates of the facility above.

CHAPTER 4

The old bull was dying slowly. His heavy, labored breathing was wet with choking blood as his cooked insides began to break apart.

He was beyond being a threat, but the mother rex avoided him anyway – his death-throes might go on for hours, and he still had a hundred tons to kick around.

There was no need to take the risk or make the effort when there was literally mountains of free meat for the taking.

Except that wasn't quite true. The Matron understood instinctively that there was no such thing as a free meal, even in the Cretaceous.

For one thing, it brought them within range of the IC-facility.

The Matron had been aware of the alien presence for some time, but hostilities had broken out only recently – mostly because, until now, the IC operations had been in the southern continents.

'*Aliens*' had never actually been there – not organisms, anyway. The extraterrestrial activity on the planet was all automation. That was one of the selling points to the organics – their operations involved no invasive species risk, not even bacteria.

They *did* tear the hell out of the land, though, and the toxic gases they released from the volcanoes were just as indigenous as any other metabolic aerosol poison, covering large swaths of the environment. Thermal activity was way up in the area as well.

But the Matron rex didn't make those associations with the newcomers – what *she* remembered was the IC had killed her mate.

That was enough to know they were dangerous.

It was also enough that she was laying for them.

Tyrannosaurs were still new on the Oracle's radar – the cull in the old valley was based on a single skirmish with the rogue male rex, but it wasn't about targeting the entire species... yet.

Since some bad incidents in the south involving big sauropods, the Oracle had sent out surveillance-bots to monitor the more troublesome indigenous life. Any large herd of titanosaurs within a hundred miles of IC-facilities could count on a pack of hovering drones following them like buzzing bees, recording their every moment.

Sauropods had been on a direct-persecution schedule for a while, now. That policy had not yet been applied to *T. rex* – not after just the one incident with the rogue.

T. rex was a large animal, but not in sauropod-category, and therefore not deemed a threat.

This again demonstrated how a computer could underestimate an opponent, and how an artificial intelligence can suffer arrogance, by not deigning to recognize a lower form as such.

It turned out a big rex could do a great deal of damage when so motivated – *way* outside its weight-class – easily comparable to what a sauropod might do.

The IC had not, to this point, given a rex a reason to come after them. The rogue rex in the last valley had been taken in a surprise raid, after it destroyed a pair of scout-drones. Beyond that, there had been no overriding feud.

Today, that changed forever. And with a *T. rex*, forever meant *forever.*

The Matron had been leading her pack cautiously along the path at the base of the cliff. They were in stalking mode – even five and six-ton adults could move with surprising stealth when they so chose. Indigo was close on the Matron's heels, the Triplets fanning to either side.

Typically, the Triplets, still lighter and faster, would run ahead and flush the game, be it ceratopsian or hadrosaur, and get them running into the jaws of the larger adults.

A hadrosaur, you hit coming at you. A trike, you waited for them to pass and then bit them in the ass.

Sauropods, you ankle-bit. A rex could take out an adult titanosaur with a single bite that severed the tendon, much the way wolverines kill moose and reindeer.

Although, that was not necessary today.

Overhead, IC-survey-bots circled over the slaughtered titanosaurs, hovering specifically over the still-struggling old bull.

Indigo and the Triplets growled nervously. The Matron grunted, ordering the pack back. There was no need for a skirmish, if it could be avoided. The mother rex watched for the survey-bots to leave.

They might have eventually, once the old bull titanosaur expired. In previous culls, they simply left the butchered carcasses to be consumed by the environment, and that meant predators scavenging.

But the Matron rex sensed that, in the immediate aftermath of the cull, the IC-drones' hackles would be up, and so she waited.

It was Varmint that set everything off.

The little rat had somehow appeared on their heels – one of his labyrinth of tunnels under the surface must have led up to the cliff-side.

And when he let out his wild, screeching alarm, it reeked of deliberate, vindictive action.

Varmint *hated* the rex and all theropods in general. He and his mammalian-kin were traditionally the prey of the ostrich-mimics and their sister-group, the sickle-clawed dromaeosaurs – both of them coelurosaurs.

Of course, because these days, *T. rex* had to hog *all* the hunter's niches, Varmint had also gotten a lot of predatory attention from juvenile tyrannosaurs.

In fact, itself a descendant of the cat-sized coelurosaur-carnosaurs, *T. rex* was the only large theropod from the group that evolved specifically to hunt humanity's small, rat-like mammalian ancestors. Coelurosaurs were actually several million years ahead of evolving snakes to target that specific prey-base.

All Varmint knew was that he despised the big dragon beasts, and passed up no opportunity to show it.

Today, he screeched his clarion-call, hollering bloody-murder, as the rex-pack tried to move under the radar of the IC-survey-bots.

CHAPTER 5

The automatic sentry guns mounted along the facility border fence sprang to life, picking out the stalking tyrannosaurs as they circled the titanosaur corpses. Unlike the hovercrafts, these were armed with simple projectile weapons, although fired via an energy charge to maximize velocity.

They opened fire into the rex pack.

The Matron had already seen the rogue put down. Her seasonal mate had been the most powerful predator in two-hundred miles, defending the territory from all comers, including other big males, for more than ten years.

That fact alone should have made the Matron skittish.

Instead, it meant she was laying for them.

The Matron... *missed* her mate – and she associated the IC with her loss.

T. rex had a primitive brain by modern hominid standards, but it was an important jump in evolution at the time – adapting the ability to *care*.

Tyrannosaurs were the first big theropods to develop true pair-bonding, like some types of ground birds. The smaller and more primitive tyrannosaurs showed a similar social structure, where the mature males typically ran alone, but would sometimes father several nests a season.

With bigger tyrannosaurs, exceeding two-tons, like Gorgosaurus and Albertosaurus, or the even larger Daspletosaurus, first of the really heavy-duty tyrant-dinosaurs, you started seeing cases of pair-bonding with the same mates over several seasons, or even a lifetime.

By the time *T. rex* rolled around, it was typical for the rogue to have a seasonal mate – usually the dominant female. It was the social-adaptation of a super-predator. The rogue's claim was absolute. And it kept him from killing every other male of breeding age in the territory. That was helpful in encouraging genetic diversity – all the more important in an ecosystem that was becoming a bit too specialized.

That was another thing that was different from just a few million years ago. Once there were different species. In the way modern Africa has more than one big cat – there are lions, leopards, as well as cheetahs – likewise, tyrannosaurs had the slender speedy Gorgosaurus cheetah, that shared a habitat with the robust lion-like Daspletosaurus.

But in the Late-late Cretaceous, there was only one.

T. rex wasn't just top-predator. It was every other niche too.

Hatchlings were born dangerous, and youngsters competed with dromaeosaurs at every stage, until they simply outgrew them.

Likewise, *T. rex* took care of most of the predatory/scavenging duties on the plains, eating the majority of a carcass, leaving minimal scraps for any starving crocs that might still be trying to make a living off the riverbanks.

All told, *T. rex* had a pugnacious approach to competition.

Put in proximity with the IC operations, there was inevitably going to be conflict.

It might, however, not have been today.

When Varmint sounded the alarm, the sentry guns were already operating under the zero-tolerance protocol activated by the presence of the titanosaurs.

The Matron felt the first blast of munitions tear into her, opening up her side and hip.

Beside her, Indigo bellowed as she was hit by a second blast, and then the Triplets.

The Matron staggered, torn between the instinct to retreat, and her protective instincts, around her sister and offspring. At her feet, the hatchlings were panicked.

Then the munitions found them as well.

A blast of Gatling-fire blew the two sisters off their feet. Little Diablo screamed aloud before a glancing shot knocked him spinning as well.

The two sisters had been blasted into bloody pieces.

For a heartbeat, the Matron stared down at her murdered children.

Then, without formality, she turned and charged the facility.

There was a difference in the movements of a predator – at six-tons, sheer mass made it dangerous for a big female rex like the Matron to push it much past twenty-five-miles an hour – not that they *wouldn't* – but the deceptive factor was acceleration. Their bodies were naturally postured like a multi-ton sprinter poised at the starter's blocks.

The Matron rex exploded forward, jaws agape, and even the automated sentry-guns seemed momentarily taken aback.

She hit the gate at a full run, crumpling the metal fence like tissue.

The factory beyond was built into the deep cavern that split the cliff. The Matron's bellows echoed off the rock walls as she burst inside.

This was the IC-munitions factory – a target that might seem inadvisable to attack face-first and head-on.

On the other hand, it was not exactly advisable to release munitions-fire within one's own weapons factory.

The Infantry's immediate response were hover-drones with energy-beams, cranked-up to burn on contact.

In the close quarters, however, the drones' maneuverability was hampered. The Matron simply charged them directly, snapping them up like soap-bubbles, even as each exploding orb splattered her face with fire and shrapnel.

Then there were accompanying roars as Indigo and the Triplets came charging in after her, picking targets more or less at random, whether it shot at them or not.

The rex pack was burned, their hides chopped and bloodied – and they were damn pissed-off about it.

Walking drones armed with projectile fire met the pack as they forced their way inside, but these were quickly smashed.

A fire had broken out within the interior machinery and was now beginning to spread.

With caution rapidly becoming a secondary concern, the IC-Infantry now implemented larger munitions.

There was a single loud, explosive blast, and Indigo was blown completely off her feet. The big female tumbled, and lay still, a fresh smoking crater caved in her side, her lifeblood flowing freely.

As the Matron turned down the main factory hall, she found herself facing a rolling tank, with a single-mounted barrel – sufficient caliber munitions to put down a rex at a shot.

Beyond caring, the Matron coiled to charge.

The weapon's cannon targeted her, zeroing-in.

Then from behind them, came a thundering bellow.

At the mouth of the cavern, stood the old bull titanosaur.

The colossus was on his feet.

There was a *whir-click* as the cannon shifted targets to the old bull.

The beast was already dying, but it was going to make its last moments count.

With a roar that shook the cavern, the titanosaur charged.

The Matron rex stepped aside as the cannon fired.

It struck the charging sauropod dead in the chest, exploding on contact.

The titanosaur let out a grunt, beginning to collapse, but its forward motion remained unchecked, its legs churning forward like massive pistons.

It reached the tank in five steps, crushing it underfoot.

The munitions within exploded all at once.

There was a moment of blindness, and the Matron was knocked off her feet. Beside her, the Triplets were also put down – one of them did not get back up.

As the Matron scrambled to her feet, more explosions began to erupt down the length of the cavern.

The titanosaur was still charging forward, even as it collapsed, burning, a dying demolition-machine, going full bore until its engine finally croaked and died.

More gun-bots turned down the main hall, opening fire – for all the good they did, because the giant sauropod's momentum carried it over all of them like an avalanche.

The Matron rex and the two surviving Triplets turned and ran for the cavern exit as another series of explosions lit up the cavern, this time more violent than before – and then they began to spread as the entire munitions store began to ignite.

Outside, Little Diablo was just regaining his own senses, staggering to his feet, looking down at his dead sisters. Then he turned to see his mother and the two Triplets come charging out of the exploding caverns as the IC-facility self-destructed.

The little rex screeched hysterically, as the Matron briefly bent to nuzzle him, before turning to look back at the burning inferno behind her.

For a moment, the Tyrant Queen seemed to smile.

Then, burned and bleeding, still smoking out of her nostrils, the Matron turned to the titanosaur banquet waiting behind her – what had now turned out to be a *hard-earned* free-meal.

Little Diablo and the two surviving sisters ran up beside the Matron, joining her as she bent and began to eat.

CHAPTER 6

The Oracle was hastily collating the data from the incident.

Operations along that entire mountain were a complete loss. Once the fire started, it just kept going – they were operating out of a volcano, after all, and the air itself was flammable.

It was a serious setback, and the Oracle was properly attentive.

Artificial intelligence necessitates emotion on some level – it's just not driven by biological needs or impulses. But even simple pragmatic thought, the gathering of information led to... opinions. And interests.

The primary 'emotion' was not dutiful concern – that was simply following its programming – the *interest* that had been stoked was chaos.

In its way, the Oracle was fascinated at how reality always differed from the model – the intervention of the random event.

Case in point was how this impossibly outmatched creature, literally a dumb beast, had actually destroyed their entire operation in the valley.

The Oracle found it frankly remarkable that any creature would attack them at all. As it understood emotion, you would more likely expect an animal to be fearful and run.

But the Oracle was learning that temperament went a long way.

There were many powerful animals the IC had encountered on a multitude of worlds that might have been able to duplicate the damage that Mother rex had done today, but the deciding factor was not just if an animal *could* – it was whether it *would*.

In this case, that rex mother had seemed to stir up the other creatures as well. That big sauropod had followed her in. Granted, it could have been acting on its own, but it was clearly responding to the incident instigated by the rex.

The Oracle had sent out surveillance drones all over the valley, and was reviewing the feed coming back, correlating it with the already-existing files on their database. It was not hard to narrow down the rex' movements, even over the course of the last several weeks.

Backtracking, the Oracle realized that this was the mate of the big male they'd just put down recently, after it had destroyed a pair of their field-units.

And even as this conclusion was being drawn, another incoming bulletin reported another attack – in this case, the surveillance-bots that had been sent to tail the rex-pack had been smashed.

The recorded footage was explanatory enough. The last thing the drone saw was a four-and-a-half-foot, tooth-studded mouth stretching wide.

It was actually quite remarkable – those surveillance-orbs were built to operate in space, but the rex had taken it out in a single chomping bite.

This same female and her pack had now been identified in two separate incidents. She had already caused far and away enough damage to be sanctioned, but this sort of demonstrated behavior might require a targeted cull.

Hopefully, a full purge wouldn't be necessary – that was both costly and destructive.

But that would be resolved going forward. For now, step-one was to put that rex and its pack down.

CHAPTER 7

The IC response was not long in coming.

Little Diablo was the first to see the lights in the sky, and then in the woods like glowing eyes.

It was just after dusk. The surviving rex-pack had eaten their fill and retreated back down into the valley.

As always, Varmint caterwauled at their approach – loud and hysterically, making sure to get all the birds squawking before disappearing down one of his labyrinth of holes.

Dakota had been waiting on the *T. rex*. The dromaeosaur-pack had made one attempt to steal up onto the dead sauropod carcasses still smoking on the hill, but had been rebuked in no uncertain terms by the Matron – she had paid for this bounty and was nowhere near ready to share. Dakota and her pack relented easily enough. They always could sneak back up once the *T. rex* went to sleep.

Now, as the rex-pack seemed headed for bed, Dakota stirred her own troops for their turn at the table.

The Triceratops herd was already settled down for the evening, gathering as a group near a grove of trees at the valley's southern perimeter. The old bull trike grumbled as the rex-pack made their way past.

No doubt the big bull heard the disturbance on the hill and likely had been watchful for anything wandering down the path from that direction. It was a dumb animal, but it learned fast enough to be wary around the IC-operation – let alone with a rex pack involved.

A rex-pack that now appeared diminished by half.

The Matron gave no obvious sign, but she was aware of the loss – her Indigo-sister, a clutch-mate who had been there literally her whole life – a nearly-grown daughter – two more hatchlings.

She retained the memory of them, the way she did of her rogue mate.

At her feet, little Diablo was likewise suddenly aware of being alone.

He had originally been one of a dozen. All but his last two sisters were killed in the raid against their father, and now they were gone too.

Diablo knew who was responsible – he didn't understand the nature of the IC, but he knew perfectly well what they had done to his family.

His mother had fought back against them today, but suffered dearly for it. They were all burned and brutalized. Little Diablo had survived a shot that killed his sisters.

The battle may have been won, but it was a costly victory – and it was only the beginning of the war.

Now the IC launched their counter-strike.

Diablo had ventured ahead of the others. Normally he was chugging at their heels, but today they were beaten and sore. Diablo had taken his own lumps but he was still just thirty-pounds, and lighter on his feet.

Thus, he saw the first walker as it came out of the trees. Saucer-shaped drones, as clear as polished glass, hovered above them, pulsing in the dark like red blinking eyes.

The walkers were simple robotic automations – fourteen-feet tall, bipedal, in order to navigate three-dimensional terrain, and outfitted with two mounted cannons for upper limbs.

Diablo's voice erupted in a screech of sufficient decibel to rouse every creature in surrounding valley. The bull trike grunted alert. Dakota and her pack pulled back into the brush.

The warning made a difference. That first walker's cannon had been aimed at little Diablo himself, but his screech alerted his mother.

Stumbling and dogged, the Matron suddenly roared back to life, charging forward at the sound of her distressed hatchlings, even as the cannons swiveled towards her.

Diablo attacked the walker's ankle like an angry Chihuahua, but he was kicked brutally aside, tumbling nearly twenty yards and lay limp.

An explosion of gunfire erupted in the Matron's face – high-velocity projectile-fire.

Flesh was chopped away from the big female's skull as her jaws smashed down on the drone's arm-cannon, piercing and crushing at the same time.

Another explosion lit up inside the Matron's jaws, flame blowing out both sides.

In a bellowing fury of pain, she ripped the walker's limb free, and stomped its mechanical carcass into scraps.

The Matron spat out burning metal, staggering back, her jaws cratered and bloody, now minus several teeth.

She was already injured, but now she was hurt.

Behind her, the two surviving Triplets roared in outrage. They both charged forward, their own jaws agape.

The walkers and the rotating orbs above them both opened fire.

Now another regiment of automations came marching out of the woods, and buzzing out of the sky – the enemy's strategy was self-evident, and brutally simple – the drones all started blasting away at every living thing in sight.

Besides every bird, lizard, rat, that also now included the herd of ceratopsians and the pack of dromaeosaurs.

The IC-policy-update had decreed the situation warranted a widespread cull, rather than a targeted one. Their facilities had taken damage on an unprecedented level, and more than one species was involved.

There were startled bellows, and then shrieks, from the trikes as munitions fire suddenly tore into the herd. From above, the floating drones began targeting individuals with high-intensity lasers, burning through their shields.

Dakota and her pack darted for cover in the rocks. Two of her daughters were dropped by cannon-fire before they made twenty-steps.

The rex-pack did their best to take the offensive. The two Triplets hit a pair of incoming walkers, face-first, their four-foot jaws both latching onto metal cannon-limbs – immediately igniting two more fiery explosions.

A second Triplet collapsed, her jaws bloody and mangled, still clinging to the demolished walker.

The last Triplet spat out a mouthful of blood and alien-wreckage. She roared defiantly, but her jaw had been broken.

In the Cretaceous, that meant she would linger and die. But today, she was still in the fight.

Now a stumbling wreck herself, the Triplet charged a third walker, even as it zeroed in on her with both its cannons.

The Triplet's skull was reinforced bone, but the high-velocity rounds penetrated deep, chopping through.

One shot hit the forward-facing eye.

The big rex staggered, careening headlong into the walker, bearing it to the ground. But then a second automation moved on her, opening fire.

The Triplet roared shrilly, stomping the first walker to scrap. Another explosion lit-up at her feet, as the cannon's power-cells burst, toppling her over.

There was a *whir-click* as the second walker's guns zeroed in.

But the Matron was there before it had a chance to fire, stomping it to the ground with both feet. But this time, she targeted the armored torso, cracking the shell. The walker was crushed like a beer can, but the impact didn't ignite the cannon's power-cells.

Predators learn.

But as the Matron turned, she saw it was too late for the last Triplet, who quivered briefly, gasping one last breath before lying still.

More walkers were moving in.

The Matron looked around, realizing she was now alone. The last Triplet was dead. Little Diablo was nowhere in sight.

Four walkers were advancing on her at once.

Above, the saucer-drones were charging-up.

Then the Matron felt a rumble in the ground and a snorting bellow.

She turned to see a charging Triceratops herd, led by the old bull.

The Matron braced, ready for an assault on both sides.

But the bellowing trike-bull led his herd thundering right on past – right into the walkers.

If a *T. rex* could look startled, the Matron did now.

The trike herd stomped all four walkers flat – each of them

igniting their cannons like mines, but the big horned beasts kept charging right over the top of them anyway – a couple of trikes rolled over dead from the blasts – brainless beasts already forgotten.

With the entire herd of Triceratops suddenly upon them – not running, not fleeing, as would be expected, but instead attacking recklessly, irreverent of returning damage, the remaining walkers were quickly overwhelmed.

The old bull trike took several direct blasts, hitting at least two cannons directly – his shield was now missing its upper right corner. But his simple nature saved him. He charged dead center, hitting the main torso, avoiding puncturing the power-cells. He learned after the first couple of times, not to trample, either – that had cost him part of a foot and a tail.

And boy, if that sonofabitch wasn't grumpy before, the Matron hadn't seen anything 'til now. The big rex was actually taken aback.

The old bull kicked like a bull in a rodeo – snorting, bellowing, going after every bipedal target he could find.

One thing about trikes – even *T. rex* wouldn't take one face-to-face. You got them running. If they ever turned back on you, especially as a group, then you damn well better stop.

T. rex' bite was a devastating *targeted* attack. But for random damage in every direction, absolutely *nothing* beat a pissed-off *Triceratops horridus* – probably the most dangerous animal at close-quarters ever.

The old bull's herd was energized, following his lead, stampeding as a herd but targeting every single walker, ignoring the hovering saucer-drones above as they began picking-off individuals with concentrated blasts.

Fire had broken out in the brush and the entire scene was lit in flickering strobe light. Explosions painted colors like blasts of thunder.

The Matron rex had actually backed-off, perhaps feeling her wounds – or because it seemed the trikes had taken point, and maybe had it handled.

It was possible this was the judgment of the IC as well.

Abruptly, the spinning saucers cut off their targeted laser

attacks.

The walkers were not down yet – the battle with the trikes was not yet decided. But the IC had apparently recommended liquidation.

Overhead, the drones were now spreading over the battle, gridlocking the entire grazing field, and they began to glow.

The Matron rex stood, looking up, calm and impassive in the way instinctual creatures are, but still aware of her own throbbing pain, and freshly conscious of the sudden loss of her entire pack.

Above her, the drones were out of reach – but they weren't attacking.

Instead, they pulsed – red, blinking lights.

The pulse-beat seemed to match the throb of pain pumping through the Matron's whole body, as the big rex' heartbeat counted one blink at a time.

Counting down...

There was a single bright light as all the drones together suddenly shone blinding red.

A second later, they detonated.

The valley below the mountain was destroyed.

CHAPTER 8

The survey-bots scanned the ravaged battlefield landscape. The Oracle wanted everything recorded.

This project was not going well, so far.

Never had the IC seen a case of animals of different species, particularly prey animals and predators, aligned against them with such fortitude.

Perhaps 'aligned' was too advanced a term – call it acting out against a common threat.

But the Mother rex had clearly inspired it. It was one thing that the Matron's own troops followed her – it was quite another when it was a herd of ceratopsians, not to mention a giant titanosaur.

And this had not been a stampede on the trikes' part. A stampede was out of fear – this was a rampage.

Ironically, the entire T. rex' game-plan in hunting Triceratops was to panic them into running.

Today, this Tyrant Queen had turned that fear into anger – and retaliation.

The Oracle was only now beginning to perceive the unique nature of Earth's Late-late Cretaceous-ecology. T. rex was the ruler – it was dominant over its environment in a way no animal ever was before – and would not be again until the advent of hominid evolution.

You saw it in the way every other animal was forced to adapt around it – shaped around it. Triceratops' shield covered its neck from a T. rex' jaws. Its horns were aimed unerringly at its belly and throat. Ankylosaurus' tail and spikes were aimed at a tyrannosaur's shins. A hadrosaur's whole body was designed for a horse-kick right in its face.

And T. rex occupied all the predator niches. From the moment it hatched, it competed with the smaller sickle-claws. And once they grew past the six-to-seven-hundred-pound dromaeosaurs, or maybe a fifteen-hundred-pound to a ton worth of crocodile, there simply *weren't* any other predators.

But a rex-pack never had the sheer size of a titanosaur. What now when they had a big one following their lead?

Or for that matter, an entire herd of like-sized horned-tanks like Triceratops, that were specifically designed to kill them?

Did that translate to a primitive form of leadership?

Many animals had alphas that others of its own pack would follow, but not inter-species.

And in most cases with alphas, if you took them out, the rest of the pack would back off. Apparently, not here. They had taken down that aggressive male in the last valley, but instead of solving the problem, it seemed to have brought down the ire of the rest of the pack.

It all represented very notable exceptions to rules the IC had recorded on over a thousand planets, just like this.

And the Oracle had never seen any example anywhere of non-sentient animals showing indications of being... what?

Inspired?

That was a *thing* with organics, but one the Oracle would not have attributed to life-forms of this evolutionary-level of mental-development.

This was still a primitive planet – that early stage all life-bearing worlds seem to go through – the rule of the dragon. That is to say, by tooth and claw, where the biggest, most powerful dominate. It was the last stage of physical evolution before intelligence began to settle in – once the dragon couldn't get any bigger or badder, brains made the difference.

In the case of organics, this intellectual development went hand-in-hand with the process of socialization. It was a necessary control mechanism, in higher-sentients – the only thing that kept weapons of mass-destruction at bay.

Because the appetite for tooth and claw never seemed to fully recede – hence, the interstellar market for pit-fighting was a constant.

On the side, the Oracle was running simulations on that front as well.

In the totality of pragmatism that comes with artificial intelligence, the Oracle compartmentalized the cut-your-losses opportunities there.

The IC had actually already introduced sauropods to the circuit – they'd been dealing with titanosaurs on the southern continent for a while, but now the Oracle was considering *T. rex* as an even more viable prospect.

They were already running simulations, estimating probabilities based on demonstrated capabilities, physical make-up and, of course, temperament. The Alamosaurus had done well in such simulations and had been introduced successfully into the circuit.

But this mother *T. rex* by herself had done more damage than any single animal, anywhere near her size. And her size was not inconsiderable – she was not as big as a sauropod, but wasn't at a disadvantage when the two were paired in simulation – one-shot battles, actually, with the rex simply biting out the tendon that supported the leg.

Based on projections, and real-world performances of the sauropods on the circuit, a rex might actually be powerful enough to compete outside the non-enhanced leagues, into the open circuit where genetic-manipulation was actually allowed.

Truthfully, as a general audience, organics didn't really care about the enhancements – any sport is better with steroids – but there was always a market for purists.

It was actually sort of a double-A league, where natural forms from different myriad worlds were scouted for raw potential, and then souped-up with wings, or poison, or growth-enhancement. Even electric-eel-like shocks.

Sauropods were still new on the circuit, and the IC had not yet fully explored their potential, but the genome-starting-point was already impressive enough. You didn't see too many hundred-ton terrestrial organisms, all gravity considerations being equal.

And that was *pre*-enhancement.

There was actually no particular limit to the degree of mutation allowed in the open-leagues, although there was extremely tight regulation of the mutagenic material itself – possible because the technology existed almost exclusively in IC hands.

Even localized outlets of the IC, like the Oracle itself, were extremely limited in what mutagen-tech they were authorized to employ. It involved some of the most deadly (and expensive!) substances known – first of all, consisting of poisons capable of breaking down DNA, and chemicals likewise toxic enough to cause mutation at that level – let alone precise enough to produce the specifically desired mutations.

Mutagens had all kinds of uses. They could be a steroid, as they were most commonly employed via the gaming-circuit.

Or they could be made into a devastating biological weapon, as was being done here – highly illegal among organics, and so the IC assured them it was never, *ever* being done.

But priorities with on-planet operations were always about harvesting vital-resources. Everything else was a distant, unconsidered second.

This localized clearance was only the beginning. The IC had decreed that immediate focus must be on getting this troublesome population under control. No more incidents would be tolerated.

Deterrents hadn't worked, so it was time for a widespread cull, throughout the entire region.

Mutagens would not yet be authorized, but the Oracle already had been running a number of genetic-designs through the simulator – considering some, rejecting others.

One option was a killer virus. Unfortunately, this tended to be difficult to narrow to a particular species or population. It also tended to be slow.

Then there was the problematically healthy metabolism of their targeted-species. Tyrannosaurs demonstrated remarkable healing abilities, surviving the loss of tails, or broken limbs that would be crippling to most wild animals, let alone a seven-ton biped.

They bounced back from infection and viruses too – their antibodies were really quite hearty.

In fact, *all* the fauna that shared the habitat showed a markedly stubborn inclination for survival. Many creatures on the landscape bore hideous scars – there were hadrosaurs that survived hollowed-out bites in the rear-quarters – *ass-to* – from a T. rex, and there were a lot of trikes with missing horns and shields – and there was more than one ankylosaur moving around on three legs.

Suffice to say, they would suck it up for a runny nose.

In the end, when widespread culls became necessary, the simplest methods were also the easiest – just go out and kill them directly.

Today, simple bombs had done the trick. That wasn't something you generally wanted to do around your own equipment, but pretty much everything locally had already been trashed.

It was evident that this northern region was going to be a costly harvest. The planet was especially rich here, so the IC considered the expense justified.

Policy was also being adopted to be a little more proactive in their clearance operations.

That was certainly justified. On an intellectual level, the Oracle was frankly astonished at the damage that had been done in this single incident. From the demolition in the cavern mining facility, to the debacle on the battlefield, there was nothing like it on the records of a thousand IC planet-side operations. The IC never had *military* operations that had gone so poorly. In point of fact, the Overmind was keeping the incident hush-hush, lest the negative publicity undercut the IC's weapons market.

From an analytical perspective, the Oracle found the incident most fascinating, in that the rex-pack's aggression had carried over to the other beasts – *prey* beasts.

Affirmative evidence that the energy in this particular cull was not wasted.

This mother rex was demonstrating behavior that indicated a pivotal point in her species' evolution – actual social influence.

Clearly, that was something that needed nipped in the bud.

T. rex had just promoted itself to zero-tolerance status. And it had taken the trike-herds with it.

As the survey-bot hovered over the charred battlefield, there was a sudden beep as its motion-detector went off.

Its 360-degree eye caught scampering movement. Over in the corner, it spotted the little mammal – the Varmint – gnawing at one of the trike corpses.

The little rat stepped out of the way just as the orb fired an energy blast. The little creature squawked, and then disappeared down its hole.

There was the crackle of flame as the foliage burned behind the missed shot. The Oracle raised a set of electronic eye-brows – that little critter had been dead in its sights, and dodged the blast.

The Oracle knew the local saurians hated those little rats – they were known to pillage nests.

In moments of independent thought separate from its programming, the Oracle could relate to that sense of revulsion. That creature poking around, chittering up so cheekily, instilled the near-emotional urge to keep the orb's lasers going until they found it, even though it was a waste of energy for a minimal threat.

The Oracle found the little rat... *creepy.*

They were not, however, the primary focus.

The problem before it was that the richest mining lay in the mountains. Tyrannosaurs lived in the surrounding lowlands, all up and down the coast, right where the IC would be needing to operate. This would be the case for the entire stretch of the northern continent.

They would be needing to plan for those eventualities.

A short-term cull was enough for now, but the Oracle knew there needed to be long-term strategies implemented for years ahead.

There was another loud beep, as the motion-detector went off again.

That little rat had found one of the downed orbs and was mugging at its camera.

The circling orb zeroed in on it and fired another shot.

But that damned little rat ducked down its hole and the blast missed again, lighting the leaves behind it ablaze.

If it had a face, the Oracle would have frowned.

That was twice. The first could be happenstance, but that little critter had stepped aside that second time like it was baiting – a mongoose dodging a cobra.

For a moment, Varmint's head popped back out of his hole, chittering cheekily. Then he disappeared.

The orb hovered, as the Oracle paused indecisively, tempted to chase the little rat down.

Then, perhaps a bit disgruntled, the orb relented.

It moved over the trike-herd, sending down a beam of light, singling out the remains of the old bull.

There was an electric glow and the dead trike seemed to glow from inside, its skeleton visible through the rough, scaly skin, as the orb recorded its entire physical being. It also took several blood samples.

Then the light-beam found the body of the dead Matron *T. rex*.

Likewise, the beam stabbed her, lit her up, creating a digitized copy down to the DNA.

The craft circled the field, taking a few more samples – another couple trikes, a dead ankylosaur, a couple of barbecued crocs and sickle-claws.

Then, once the entire site was recorded for posterity, the orbs all pulled back, and as a flock, they retreated, shooting straight up into the night sky. In moments, they were just another cluster of blinking lights, indistinguishable among the night's stars.

On the ground below, the forest burned.

CHAPTER 9

Diablo remembered Dakota – he knew she and his mother weren't friends.

The dromaeosaur mother stared back at him from the other end of the hollow log, where the two of them had ridden out the storm. Her own pack had variously been obliterated by cannon-fire or charcoaled by heat-beams. Dakota herself had gone to ground or she wouldn't have survived the drone detonations.

Diablo had been knocked unconscious early on, but came-to during the last blitz, retreating under the same log, which was, fortunately, old and petrified, with a couple seasons of hardening under regular coats of volcanic ash.

Dakota had hissed at him as he abruptly joined her under the half-buried log, and might have made an issue of it, except that was when the drones had all gone off.

Even with the protection of the log, the blast was near fatal – heat whistling through like a giant wooden kazoo, and the sheer shock-impact was stunning.

Diablo must have been knocked unconscious again, or at least settled in to a semi-stunned stupor, and perhaps dozed, because when he blinked suddenly awake, it was morning.

Dakota was already up, clawing her way out from under the old log.

Part of it had burned. It had also rolled, and been partly crushed, as well as broken in the middle. A little more either way and it would probably have killed one of them.

Cautiously, Diablo poked his nose out, scenting the air, before hopping up out into the open.

Dakota glanced back at him warily. He wasn't big, but he was still a rex. On another day, she would have already killed him.

At the moment, she was more concerned looking for her remaining brood.

It took about ten minutes to separate the remains of each of them, identifiable by scent.

Diablo, meanwhile, had no trouble finding his mother.

The Matron lay where she had fallen, her body broken and burned. Six-tons of her.

Diablo hooted – that shrill infant-hoot that always brought the adults of his species running, be it his mother, or his aunts and adult sisters.

Today there was nothing. There was not even the answering cries of birds. The entire valley was subdued.

Or 'dead', might be a better description.

Diablo stood by the body of his mother for maybe half-an-hour. But battered and parched himself, he finally made his way down to the water.

Dakota was already there, standing knee-deep in the incoming surf, nursing abrasions and burns. Her head was perked and wary, her eye out for crocs – normally a big risk at the shore, especially in the early morning glare as the sun rose up over the water.

Today was even worse – the water was full of smoke and soot, cloudy and camouflaging.

The crocs, however, did not seem much in evidence today.

When Diablo touched his lips to the water, he found it hot, like dishwater – as if it had been super-heated and then cooled over the last several hours.

That would explain no crocs.

Diablo glanced up and down the beach. Besides himself and the mother sickle-claw, there seemed to literally be nothing else alive.

Then he heard a chittering and saw Varmint, his back to them, already gnawing away at the leg of a fallen ceratopsian.

The little rat perked his head, glancing back at the two theropods at the water's edge – coelurosaurs, the both of them – not much loved by the mammalian-class. Then he bent back to eat.

Diablo and Dakota glanced at each other, and with the saurian equivalent of a shrug, they both made their way back up the beach to the waiting carrion.

No such thing as a free meal, even in the Cretaceous.

This meal wasn't free.

Dakota hissed threateningly when Diablo sniffed at the remains of her brood, and he likewise growled a warning when she poked around the burnt remains of his mother.

There was no reason to engage. Dakota had simply hopped off, darting over to one of the ceratopsians. And Diablo had promptly found one of his own. It wasn't as if there weren't literally tons of food right there for the taking.

It was, however, a significant moment, because it represented one of the most fundamental elements of socialization among higher predators – the ability to learn what is *not* food.

A crocodile could never learn that. Nor could a more primitive carnosaur.

Dromaeosaurs and tyrannosaurs, however, were both coelurosaurs – a more advanced, derived group of theropods. *T. rex* was actually an intellectual, as dinosaurs went – it had the single largest brain in the dinosaur kingdom. Proportionally, Dakota's brain-case was slightly smaller, but as a close relative of evolving birds, she was more pack – or flock – oriented. She was particularly responsive and evocative of sounds, with a vocal acuity that could have mimicked human speech, like a parrot, if she could have heard it.

At the moment, Diablo and Dakota still saw each other as rivals – not a threat with food aplenty, and so were tolerant of each other as long as neither went territorial – and with both their entire packs gone, this was not a pressing impulse for either one of them.

On the other hand, both had recently experienced loss of companions and pack-members, and they both had enough brains to miss them. In their own way, they were grieving, and recognized that they both had been there.

And when the survey-bot came through on its morning rounds, they both remembered who had done it.

This was not food either. Neither was this a rival.

It was the *enemy*.

A *common* enemy.

At the first sound of the buzzing drone, Dakota and Diablo first went rigid, and then darted for cover, huddling together beneath the severed shield of a decapitated Triceratops. There was a frustrated chittering as Varmint abandoned his trike-leg, and darted down his hole.

Diablo had instinctively gone under Dakota's wing like a frightened duckling. Dakota accepted him under her arm, like one of her lost chicks.

The floating orb above seemed to be doing a survey count, scanning each individual corpse, as if making sure every last beast was dead.

As it hovered above, Diablo found the red glow in its marble center matched in his own eye.

Predators were good estimators of size – as in, 'am I big enough to kill that?'.

The orb was roughly two-feet across. To Diablo's eye, that was just his size.

But as he started to move, Dakota beat him to it.

The mother dromaeosaur leaped, snatching the drone with outstretched claws and digging with the sickles on both feet.

For a moment, the drone hovered in midair, as if startled. Dakota weighed more than six-hundred-pounds and the orb tumbled briefly before adjusting its gravity.

But that was when Diablo jumped in – a bit chagrined at getting there late, he charged headfirst...

… basically smacking his face against the dome, with jaws not wide enough to get around it.

But the impact knocked it off-center and Dakota wrestled on top of it, bearing it to the ground. Its claws scratched the glass, and might have pierced it given time, but Diablo was bound and determined to help, moving in now with stomping feet, pummeling the orb into the volcanic ground.

Something, be it the digging sickles or stomping rex-hooves, or both together, cracked the shield.

The initial spark knocked both of them back – fortunately – as an instant later, the drone's power-cells burst.

Both Diablo and Dakota were scorched and peppered with diamond-shards of shrapnel, and sent spinning.

But they also both got back to their feet.

The two of them staggered, exchanging brief glances, before both jumping, startled, at a sudden squawk from behind.

Varmint was already peeking out of his hole, eyeing his abandoned trike-leg.

Dakota and Diablo looked down at the smoking, ruined drone, and then they turned back to the piles of carrion still waiting.

This metal thing on the ground wasn't food. But *this* was.

And they had it all to themselves. Minus an irritating rat.

It was hard won.

They were both well-fed for that first couple of weeks together.

That helped a lot at the beginning.

CHAPTER 10

It wasn't long before the unlikely pair gained a kind of notoriety among the Cretaceous landscape. The combined scents of two big-game predators traveling together heightened the nerves among herd animals, and they were thus, more likely to panic and run if you jumped out of the bushes and yelled, *BOO!*

And working together as hunters, that was basically their entire strategy – especially at the beginning when Diablo was still small.

Early on, yelling *BOO!* was Diablo's job. Dakota picked out their targets, always something within the size-range the sturdy female sickle-claw could bring down. But once he'd flushed the prey, Diablo always took a bite – *always* – while it was still kicking.

He made sure to participate in the kill.

Normally, a male rex orphaned in the wild would have simply died. He wouldn't normally have been adopted by another rex any more than by a sickle-claw, and he was not old enough to fend for himself.

But Dakota was a longtime pack-leader, who knew how to delegate her team's strengths. Having lost the rest of her pack, she recognized that even an infant rex was not without tools.

A baby Tyrannosaurus still bit damn hard. They were also instinctively strategic hunters, even more so than the crafty sickle-claws, and Diablo responded quickly to Dakota's teachings.

Their attack strategies were based on their own body-types, but were not altogether at odds. Both were ambush-hunters, and bore weapons of killing far out of proportion to their weight. Diablo had his jaws. Dakota had that wicked ten-inch foot-sickle. Both designed to kill large prey, and do so unequivocally.

Dakota's slashing claw was more gaudy, and arguably more cruel.

But the bite of *T. rex* was more absolute. *Nothing* survived a full-hit from those chomping, guillotine jaws.

Of course, Diablo was still little, and even working together, in the Late-late Cretaceous world, that did not make the two of them Varsity.

They were still stragglers – survivors.

Although, it got better once Diablo started getting older and could pull more of his weight.

And a young tyrannosaur grew fast. By his second birthday, he already matched Dakota's size, and was growing every day.

The pair of them made a formidable team, developing unique strategies for different prey that took advantage of both their strengths, while compensating for their weak-points.

Ankylosaurs, for example, were always trouble-spots for tyrannosaurs – a high-risk, low-yield prey-item, that had an odds-on chance of leaving an attacker with long, slender shins crippled.

But with Dakota, Diablo learned new ways of going about it.

Experienced adult *T. rex*, like the Matron, basically stomped ankylosaurs to death. She would pin them to the ground so they couldn't twist their spikes and club-tail into her legs, and then she'd crack their shell.

But that required weight, and Diablo wasn't there yet. But living in the shadow of tyrannosaurs, the local dromaeosaurs had become ankylosaur specialists.

Dakota's approach was actually similar to old-style carnosaurs attacking giant sauropods – running in and cutting a big, slow opponent. A big bull *Ankylosaurus magniventris* could go three-tons versus a Dakota raptor's seven-hundred-pounds.

But those scythe claws were at least as crippling by pound as those big carcharodonts of yesteryear, delivering long gaping, open slices.

The trick was to remember to let go and retreat, rather than hang on, digging in for more with repeated bicycle kicks, which sickle-claws were prone to do – a method more effective on hadrosaurs.

But you could take out a big ankylosaur by hamstringing the leg. Sometimes you had to wait a minute for them to expire – they were hearty animals that could bleed out over days, or starve over a period of weeks.

There was also the problem that sometimes they died on their stomach, with all that meat still covered by the shell. A big rex could simply flip it over, and break through the less-armored belly.

In fact, Dakota had sometimes utilized tyrannosaurs for just that purpose – like a can-opener. She knew the Matron from the old valley, and spoiled by the fat, plump hadrosaurs, she and the other *T. rex* tended to minimize their attention to armored dinosaur carcasses.

If Dakota and her pack brought down a hadrosaur in scent range of the Matron, the rex pack would take it. With an ankylosaur, they would sometimes take the trouble of cracking it open to get the easy guts, but the rest of the meat was buried in bone. Even though a rex had bone-shearing teeth, it tended to just *be* mouthfuls of bone, so they soon left it alone.

But for a tiger-sized sickle-claw, or still-growing youngster *T. rex,* gnawing between the bones of an elephant-sized carcass was doable.

Pint-sized tyrannosaur-jaws were also still the size of a typical predatory shark. They could quite effectively mimic the dromaeosaur's attack strategy on ankylosaurs. It was just, as hatchlings, it never came up. By the time they got big enough to hunt on their own, they were too tall to duck under an armored dinosaur's spikes to get at the legs. Stomping, then, was the only option, unless you wanted to break your teeth on the back shell.

Of course, ceratopsians were still the most dangerous prey. But again, Dakota and Diablo managed to put together an attack-plan that utilized both their talents.

Simple things worked against each prey-animal's defense. Triceratops was damn-near impregnable coming from the front. Therefore, always approach from the back.

The problem with that was, Triceratops was built to turn on a dime. If that shot from the back didn't do the job, there were six-foot horns being whipped around, angrily, with upwards of eight-tons behind it.

Trikes were also extremely quick over short distances – they could explode in bursts of speed that beat any rhino.

But they were short-winded. That explosive movement was costly, and after their initial charge, they tended to stand and posture, rather than actively chase.

That was when Dakota and Diablo would go to work.

First they would separate their target – as an experienced hunter, Dakota always found the one with the limp – preferably, an aging bull, with enough attitude to be baited.

Once you got them running, you separated the limper off. Diablo was good at that. He wasn't big enough to take on even a wounded trike face-to-face, yet, but he could talk-trash with the best of them.

Diablo would rush in as the gimpy trike thundered past, snapping at its haunches, like an adult. The trike would invariably pivot, and face him off.

This was where Diablo would posture, roaring like he was twenty-feet-tall and seven-tons like his daddy, instead of this seven-hundred-pound litter-runt, with attitude.

The trike would typically posture back – and then, at the very moment it started to charge, that was when Dakota attacked from the back – not so big a bite as a mama *T. rex*, but with an unguarded strike, she could hamstring a trike just fine – always remembering to dash immediately away rather than hang-on, using the trike's own forward momentum to give her the window to get in and out.

Then they would go back-and-forth. The trike would charge after Dakota on its now-injured leg, exposing its backside to Diablo, who would take his own bite – again immediately retreating.

Two or three of those, and the trike would usually drop, bleeding out within the hour.

But more notably, and what would ultimately prove more significant long-term, Diablo and Dakota had also taken to targeting IC-equipment wherever they found it – be it survey-drones, or transport-bots – they knocked-over storage receptacles and kicked over fences.

Drones required a touch, as well. They had a tendency to explode if you ruptured their power-cells. They also had 360-degree vision, so an ambush attack had to be instantaneous. If they saw you coming, they might kill you. *Or* they might call a bunch of their friends.

Walkers were easy, so long as you kept within Dakota's size-range. You took out their joints, stomped their headless torsos, and cracked their shells – *those* guys didn't explode unless you ruptured one of their cannons.

Predators learn fast. And they learn faster once they've seen their kin slaughtered.

Diablo and Dakota made a sport of it. Never being obvious, never establishing a pattern the IC could track. Their nomadic path took them across the Lamamidian continent of Cretaceous North America over the changing seasons, following game, while avoiding the local predators, be they rex or raptor, who didn't take kindly to strangers on their hunting grounds.

So they were already keeping a low profile from the general population. That made it difficult for the IC to pinpoint them.

It also kept them out of the way of the culls that tended to sprout whenever IC-gear was taken out.

And those culls were continuing to happen. As they made their meandering path north and west, Diablo and Dakota learned to watch for the signs.

There were always scouts – survey-bots – sometimes walkers, most often those flying little orbs, buzzing among the herd-beasts, mapping the terrain. They weren't recognizance missions – they were laying out territory for the next mining operation.

After the loss the IC experienced with the Matron's attack on a completed-installation, the cull now came *before* the construction of the facility.

So now, when those survey-bots appeared, Dakota and Diablo went into their guerrilla-mode. Knowing the cull was coming, they started taking out as many of those damned drones as they could. And they weren't hard to spot – they made no particular attempt at stealth. But most of the beasts just ignored them. The drones had actually come to expect that, which left them somewhat vulnerable to Dakota and Diablo's depredations.

Once the rex/raptor duo had taken-out a number of these automations, they would retreat from the area. When the IC responded, they would already be long gone.

Interestingly enough, along their travels, they also picked-up an unlikely hitchhiker.

Varmint had migrated right along with them, keeping

deliberately to the same general path.

Mammals might be vermin, but they weren't stupid. Varmint learned from experience too, and he'd discovered following Dakota and Diablo's movements from valley to valley kept him out of the way of the IC.

It actually offended the little rat on general principles, especially, with Dakota on the team – because, while he might hate *T. rex*, he *really* hated dromacosaurs. Not Dakotaraptor, so much, but those little wolf and coyote-sized bastards who *ate* guys like him. But as far as Varmint was concerned, it was guilt by association.

On the other hand, he was happy to ride Diablo and Dakota's coattails.

The truth was, most of the animals were on the move. The culls were having the desired effect – the indigenous fauna that survived was clearing out. The ceratopsians had been added to the IC's zero-tolerance list, and that accounted for the top herbivore in the northern ecosystem.

Of course, ankylosaurs and hadrosaurs, and other non-targeted beasts tended to get culled with them, but that was pretty much non-specified-agenda anyway.

Dakota and Diablo sometimes hovered at the perimeter after these culls, just to take advantage of the carrion, although this was hairy because the IC had taken to pot-shotting wandering scavengers after a raid. They were looking for one-hundred-percent clearance, after all.

But as seasons turned into years, the continued IC-activity drove the rex/raptor duo further and further north, eventually out of the southern valleys that had been *T. rex* territory for two-and-a-half-million years.

Diablo didn't know all that, but he recognized that he was being driven out. He also knew who was making it happen – the same ones who killed his mother.

He damn-well held it against them too.

That was going to be a problem for the IC down the line because, as he grew, his territorial-instinct and alpha-aggression would grow with it.

Diablo was laying for them.

And a *T. rex never* forgot.

CHAPTER 11

Dakota mated periodically over the intervening years.

It was actually traumatic for poor Diablo the first time, because she just up and vanished, leaving him panicked and alone, before she reappeared a week later – freshly knocked-up.

Then came the eggs, and the new step-siblings.

Dakota had been extremely skittish over that first litter, hissing dangerously whenever Diablo came close.

But truthfully, there was no need. Instinctively, an elephant-sized species like *T. rex* was cautious around youngsters, and this was Diablo's pack.

He *did* learn early-on that sickle-claws were a lot more volatile than tyrannosaurs. For one, each brood started out with little brothers, but their sisters usually killed them. Only the sturdiest males survived childhood in a dromaeosaur-pack.

Diablo, for his part, got a few scratches on his nose, but his step-siblings quickly learned to tolerate his presence. In turn, their big brother didn't bite them in half.

This was another area where tyrannosaurs and sickle-claws were more compatible than one might think. Diablo behaved around his smaller step-sisters, the way he would around hatchlings – both careful and protective.

That *T. rex* guard-dog-instinct also went a long way to preserving the solidarity of Dakota's continued leadership, as she began growing older.

By the time her offspring had grown large enough to possibly challenge the six-hundred-pound mama-raptor, Diablo himself was already approaching the size of a baby elephant – still a far-cry from full seven-ton adulthood, but more of big brother than any of his sisters wanted to mess with, if it came to defending his adoptive mom.

But Diablo was protective of all his new siblings as well, although their number pared down over time. The Cretaceous world took its toll. Several died, some at each other's hands. A couple of daughters mated and left to start packs of their own. Dromaeosaurs had a 'queen bee' mentality, and the pregnant daughters would be driven out by the mothers.

By the time Dakota's first litter had fully grown, the pack was down to four – a big sister, nearly six hundred pounds, who sported a purplish plume on her head, was the one responsible for most of the scratches on Diablo's nose. She had proven to be a lifer because her sheer aggression actually prevented her from mating. She was also one of the primary culprits when one of the siblings killed each other.

There were two little sisters from the next brood, full grown, but not as large, and sporting carrot-tops – likely a different father.

Then there was Baby Sister – a blond-curled teenager. She was the most demure, but put up with zero bullying from her older siblings. Even Big Sister gave her due respect.

For Diablo, they were *his* pack. And once he started getting big enough, they actually started riding around on his back, giving him the appearance of a spiny plumed spine, and a feathered headdress.

That became how they traveled when going long distance – which was regularly. Besides the continuing encroachment of the IC, they were forced to keep on the move.

This was one of the drawbacks of traveling with an orphaned *T. rex* – it meant they were without a home. They were not welcome anywhere they went.

Other tyrannosaur-packs were extremely sketchy about rival predators in their territory – sickle-claws *or* more *T. rex*, let alone both. It followed that Diablo had grown-up largely estranged from his own kind.

And once the young rex got his growth, beginning in his early teens, he also started attracting the negative attention of the big rogue males who guarded their territories like jealous dragons hoarding treasure. A young buck like Diablo, they would attack on sight.

It was Dakota who went a long way towards keeping young Diablo alive, because the pugnacious young rex wouldn't have backed down, likely getting himself killed.

The mother-raptor kept them on the outskirts of every territory they traveled, and stayed more or less on the move, lest her adopted son pick a fight with a seven-ton rogue.

Then, of course, now that he was getting older, there were the girls...

CHAPTER 12

A *T. rex* goes through puberty in its teens. At sixteen, Diablo was sexually mature and beginning his growth-spurt into adulthood.

And like any teenager, he was hyper-interested in the opposite sex.

Dakota had tried to steer them clear of the other rex-packs, as they moved from territory to territory. But Diablo still developed a roving eye for the young, long-legged teenage females, albeit, so far, at a distance.

It was only a matter of time before he finally encountered a real-life girl face-to-face – although you couldn't exactly call it *'meet-cute'*.

They had only been in the new valley a couple of days. They had been following a general migration of ceratopsians – Torosaurus *and* Triceratops in this case, somewhat atypically traveling together.

There had been a general exodus from the southern territories. Diablo's little tribe were not the only ones on the move.

Varmint had ridden the saurian tide, now sporting a litter of wives and kids – the group of which scampered from hole to hole, like prairie dogs, between the legs of the giant eight-ton herbivores – sometimes actually lounging on the big trikes and ankylosaurs' backs, beside the parasite-eating birds – sometimes snacking on a few of them as well.

The little rat had actually done quite well. Following in Dakota and Diablo's path, which was always just ahead of the general migration, kept them away from the IC, and well-fed just snacking on their left-overs.

Of course, every now and then, one of the sickle-clawed sisters would try and sample some Didelphodon too, but by now, Varmint was a wizened old-tom – he and his mob of kits kept to his underground sanctuary of tunnels.

Riding the trikes provided another modicum of security – although, every once in a while, a rex would try and bite its ass off, so you had to watch that you weren't sitting on *that* one. The best way was to pick the biggest and the meanest, and there was always a big mean trike bull leading every herd.

Other refugees moving north were several groups of hadrosaurs, mostly *Edmontosaurus annectens*, which typically lived much further south, were on the move with the armored and horned dinosaurs.

In the short term, from the predators' viewpoint at least, it meant good hunting.

And like always, Dakota and Diablo's little band were operating on someone else's turf.

Dakota had been leading them along the perimeter of an open field, bordering a wide river. They kept to the trees, casing the grazing-land beyond, where the herd animals were congregating in the hundreds.

The Sisters had gone-off a little half-cocked. They'd not eaten in days, and were already eyeballing a limping hadrosaur. Big Sister had run off ahead, followed by Baby Sis and the two Carrot-tops, despite Dakota's objecting bark.

It almost cost them their lives as one of the local *T. rex*, waiting in ambush, with its eye on that same limping duckbill, took umbrage.

The Sisters scattered, but the rex was already upon them. It was an adolescent female, Diablo's own age, with three-and-a-half-foot jaws that could snap a Dakotaraptor in half.

Diablo charged forward to intercede, bellowing like the mightiest rogue.

The young female turned from the Sisters, jaws agape, fangs bared, roaring dangerously.

That was when Diablo got his first look at her.

At this age, she was a little taller, but he was heavier – as a male, he would grow somewhat slower, fully mature a bit later.

But she was long-limbed and muscular – lean and shapely too.

And *wow* – green eyes.

T. rex tended towards yellow eagle-eyes, but this female's were riveting, almost emerald green.

By rex-standards, she was *hot*.

Dakota saw Diablo's sudden shift in attention as she corralled the scampering Sisters behind her. The dromaeosaur-mother hissed disapprovingly.

But that was pretty much her reaction to everything.

It was actually tyrannosaur-nature that made their enduring bond possible. Beyond the nesting-instinct that had saved little Diablo in infancy, dromaeosaur-society was a vicious hierarchy, where the pressure from below never ended.

Diablo offset all of that. Himself already weighing in at four-tons, he didn't feel dominated by his six-hundred-pound step-mother – he simply followed her lead like a Great Dane might an older poodle.

He did, however, feel a little more pressure from this female rex.

She was still in her gawky teen years, but already morphing from the sprinter juvenile to the powerful adult.

The green-eyed female might look good but they weren't friends yet. She snarled at him in no uncertain terms.

At this point, she was just facing him off – establishing territory.

But she wasn't chasing him away either.

Dakota growled a warning.

Diablo ignored her for a few vital seconds before he realized why.

Green-eyes' mother had just arrived home.

And she brought *all* her sisters and aunties with her.

Diablo turned at the outraged roar as the senior female, nearly six-tons, approaching the size of the Matron, burst into the clearing. Her own pack filed in behind her – half-a-dozen adult females.

That would have been the end of it right there, except that this was a mom-thing, and the rest of the pack held back.

The big senior female, however, moved on Diablo in full zero-tolerance mode.

Diablo made a big mistake – he treated it like a rivalry with a male. The female instead went for his throat. She would have killed him in an instant, except he realized his mistake, and turned his bony-crested skull into her incoming strike, batting her head aside in the manner of a male-joust.

That saved his neck being bitten out, and the senior female's teeth only grazed his shoulder, taking out a respectable chunk all by itself, but as she followed through on her charge, her greater weight slammed into him.

If he'd fallen, it would again have been over in moments, but he stumbled for his footing, bracing against her, being forced back by a bigger linebacker, but still on his feet.

Then he shunted her to one side and disengaged.

Diablo turned and made a break for the trees.

At that moment, Green-eyes, perhaps saving face, made a lunge at his retreating flanks, but Dakota and the Sisters all leaped up at her face, screeching wildly, before ducking quickly away from Green-eyes' snapping jaws, and darting after Diablo, fleeing into the forest.

For a moment, the senior female made as if to follow, but then relented, settling back, grunting the others to attention.

She turned to Green-eyes sternly.

The teen female bowed her head, admonished.

CHAPTER 13

The Oracle was just reviewing the latest updates from the IC-Overmind.

It seemed the Collective was raising their production-demand again. Their operation on Earth had been producing good yields, but the expense of operating so far out in the boondocks, was becoming prohibitive.

Normally, on primitive or developing planets, the IC was fairly hands-off about the local ecology, but that was window-dressing for the organic customers, when they were operating within charted space.

Out here, practicality was all that mattered. And the Oracle had just been handed a production schedule that exceeded their capacity.

Until now, they had been harvesting the planet as a steady resource – a renewable one, given patience.

The parameters of the operation, however, had now been redefined as a clear-cut. Ultimately, the planet was small, a single viable green oasis in desert-space, and the efforts to keep operations going simply were not cost effective – especially considering the unique nature of the resistance the Oracle had logged from the local indigenous wildlife.

Updated policy was to strip the place for resources and then leave.

The Oracle didn't have the option of non-compliance – or of cutting corners, or lying to the boss. They shared a brain.

As in accordance with its programming, the Oracle immediately increased operations.

But down-and-dirty clear-cuts meant resistance even from a compliant population. The Oracle knew to expect trouble. This ecology had attitude.

It planned to get ahead of it.

Again, that meant putting down animals en-mass. It also meant a large commitment of resources. The Overmind wouldn't like that. But it was what it was.

For the last several seasons, the Oracle had already been enacting a widespread depopulation scheme, as they advanced their operations up the northern continent.

It had actually been working out well. They would send in clearance-crews on the ground – these days it was usually drones with flame units. Once the targeted-species restrictions were lifted, simply burning them out was the easiest way to go. As far as the IC was concerned, it wasn't any harder to strip-mine a volcano, if the forest outside was burnt to charred ruin.

Still, they had continued to experience casualties. The *T. rex* continued to be a problem, wherever you found them, but a persistent thorn was what seemed to be an unlikely rex/dromaeosaur team that had, over the last several seasons, been consistently hitting isolated targets, most often advance scouts.

This oddball guerrilla-team moved ahead of the IC-operations, clearing out before the inevitable burn, or on-the-ground cull.

The Oracle had to admit they were a sneaky pair. It was remarkable that any of their drones, with all their sensory equipment, could even be unknowingly stalked by a dumb animal, let alone have it actually get the drop on them.

So far, there had been no greater attention given to tracking down the pair – which seemed to have grown to a *T. rex* and a *pack* of sickle-claws after the first few seasons. The damage they did was random and incidental, and the effort to target them would be wasted – if scouts were there in the first place, that meant a cull was already scheduled. The Infantry-units would keep a lookout for this particular gang, but couldn't prioritize.

But they remained elusive. None of the culls had netted them yet. They kept showing up at the next valley, as the IC continued to advance north. A single drone would go down, its last imagery a visual of gaping jaws, or sometimes a stomping foot.

The strategy the Oracle had been implementing, regarding the general cull of the rex-population, was basically bringing their numbers down with simple open slaughter. But unlike typical *T. rex* or dromaeosaurs, this particular group was nomadic, and seemed wise to the IC's pattern of movement, at least enough to recognize when to leave the territory.

There were, however, more negative returns on these culls than just those few unique incidents.

The Oracle *was* seeing evidence of aggressive behavior among other packs of tyrannosaurs.

Whether word had spread through the local animal community, or instinct traveled, they were logging more cases of *T. rex*, both individuals and packs, attacking IC-facilities and drones.

Worse, it seemed that other species were joining them. Several more incidents with sauropods had been confirmed, as well as ankylosaurs, and even hadrosaurs, although ceratopsians stood out as the most common-offenders.

The Collective did not engage in wars. It performed tactical eliminations.

It was time for a wider-cull. On the ground, Infantry-operations would be stepped up.

But the next step would be the purge.

That meant mutagens.

Preparations were already being made in the direction of that inevitability. It would take time to engineer the appropriate strains specific to the targeted population. Even though concern for collateral damage was minimal, the chemicals involved were extremely dangerous and those bottles would only be accessed in orbit, via the refinery facility, already fashioned for hazardous materials.

They had been playing with the DNA matrix-strands of the Earth beasts for a while now. In fact, several of these modifications had already been introduced into the gaming circuits.

Weaponization on a larger, military-scale was in progress. Even at that moment, significant quantities of the appropriate mutagenic chemicals were being refined – a re-purposed conveyor-belt that was now filling vials of glowing green, like plutonium, condensed into aerosol form – perhaps the deadliest substance ever known.

But that was still for the future. For the current phase, simple on-site weapons should suffice. With the goal now being to completely clear-out entire populations, not waiting for the effects of disrupting breeding, all they really needed to do in the short-term was be thorough – every last egg, every last hatchling. Advance scouts would now initiate munitions on contact with any and all indigenous wildlife. Then they would initiate a burn.

Infantry had also been working on a few new automations, and specifically, some new cybernetics.

The IC had offered recommendations based on data accumulated in the interstellar fight circuits. Because the revenue was huge, this was often where the best numbers came from – those records don't lie.

Suffice to say, in practice, their genetic-modifications had performed well.

Every creature, even *Tyrannosaurus rex*, has its weakness. In the case of a rex, you simply had to look at the world around it.

In its own environment, the biggest threats were another rex, or else something that it was trying to eat.

So the IC-Infantry had started there. Their automated war-bots specs were based on what nature had already done. The cyborg-units were also engineered with exactly the same approach, essentially checking all their opponent's advantages, and then plus-one.

As the Infantry prepared to launch its operation, the Oracle was confident it wouldn't be close this time.

CHAPTER 14

Diablo was licking his wounds when the local Big Boss rex found him.

The big male rogue easily went seven-tons, gnarled and scarred after years of defending his valley from all comers. He might even have been old enough to be Green-eyes' father. At the very least, he would likely be the senior female's seasonal mate.

In either case, Diablo's presence was not to be tolerated.

The teen rex was still walking around dreamy-eyed and distracted, squawking now and again as Dakota and the Sisters pecked at the open wound Green-eyes' mom had taken out of his shoulder – a flesh wound, that a *T. rex*' metabolism would laugh off, although another foot closer and it would have taken his whole arm.

Dakota was irritable. Her back-feathers were up. She never liked contact with rex-packs, and was not happy at all to see Diablo's burgeoning interest.

Some might call it a mother's empty-nest panic.

Dakota was more concerned about the very thing that happened next.

She remembered the old valley, and the Matron's own seasonal mate, a big bull rex that guarded his territory like a junkyard dog.

And every rex-territory had one. Intruders were not welcome.

Diablo was now big enough to count.

Dakota caught the scent first. Her stepson rex' super-nose *should* have, but his head was clouded with teenage pheromones.

The roar that reverberated through the clearing brought him back down to Earth real quick.

At the forest's edge, two trees were kicked over as the rogue made his deliberately dramatic entrance.

All across the open field, right up to the river, the grazing herds of trikes and hadrosaurs perked up, ready to run or fight.

The bellowing roar was simultaneously a reassurance and a warning. The rogue wasn't hunting today – he was there to kick somebody's ass.

His eyes found Diablo.

Without ceremony, the rogue charged.

Dakota leaped on Diablo's back, screeching into his ear – dromaeosaur-speak for "*Run Goddamnit!*"

But Diablo held his ground as the seven-ton male battened down on top of him.

Cursing horribly, Dakota leaped clear, scattering the Sisters aside as Diablo moved forward to meet the challenge.

Apparently learning nothing from tangling with the senior female, the teen rex was bound and determined to lock jaws.

To his credit, he actually went after the big rogue with every bit the Hell of his namesake. Diablo had precious little interaction with his own species since his pack had been slaughtered, but he'd held his own with his big sisters back in the day.

The big rogue actually seemed surprised, even taken-aback that this young upstart was so willing an opponent. When their jaws clamped together this combative little shit actually tried to bulldog him.

Then, before he could react properly, he suddenly had five sickle-clawed dromaeosaurs crawling all over his ass, digging in with ten-inch claws.

Now he was pissed-off.

With a wild shake, he clenched down on Diablo's jaws and flung the teen-rex aside like a four-ton barrel-toss. Bellowing angrily, he turned his jaws savagely after Dakota and the Sisters, as they swarmed him.

But rough-housing with Diablo had left them a bit more savvy to a rex' moves than your typical dromaeosaur-pack – they dodged the chomping jaws, and retreated back quickly.

Diablo was climbing painfully to his feet. *T. rex* were heavy-duty, and built for impact, but it still hurt when he landed. It had not exactly been a well-executed kimo roll.

The rogue turned back to his teen rival, his eyes glinting dangerously – he was now splashed red with his *own* blood.

Granted, Diablo's mom and little sisters accounted for most of it, but there was still going to be Hell to pay.

Dakota screeched again – exhorting – *demanding* – RUN GODDAMNIT!!

Whether it was lingering pheromones activating a mating-rivalry instinct, or perhaps simply a dumb invincible teenager, Diablo again stood his ground.

The big male paused, and actually seemed to nod approvingly, as if in due respect to the feisty youngster.

He was still going to kill him, of course.

The rogue moved forward purposefully.

Diablo braced, setting his feet.

But this time the attack came from above.

CHAPTER 15

The attack actually wasn't specifically targeting them, otherwise the first bombs probably would have killed them both.

But this incursion today was for *everybody*.

The first bombs were launched like a volley of arrows over an attacking army – which is exactly what it was.

Diablo and the rogue were both knocked over by the nearest blast.

Out on the grazing field, Varmint, who had been lounging atop one of the largest bull trikes, squealed out a hysterical and belated warning. A dozen more rats popped-up on the other trikes like gophers, all of them leaping off the ceratopsians' broad backs and diving for their holes.

Several didn't make it, and were blown apart, along with their trike mounts, into bloody puffs of fur.

Varmint saw two generations of children and grandchildren killed right in front of him. This was the first time the IC had actually caught up with them. He chittered dire maniacal epithets before disappearing, with a few ragged survivors, down his hole.

On the field up top, the carnage began.

From out of the surrounding trees came the walkers. The Infantry's first wave was basic automations.

Like simple pawns, the walkers marched into the valley, their cannon-arms firing projectile blasts into all the herd-beasts at once, even as hovercrafts circled above, picking out individual targets with high-intensity heat-beams. As they went, the flying orbs also lit the surrounding foliage ablaze, spreading the fire to accompany the walkers, as they strode through, unbothered by the flames.

Diablo knew these bastards well. At this point, he could handle a few of them on his own – mostly it was about what not to do.

Unfortunately, the rogue rex hadn't yet been schooled, and he immediately charged face-first through the cannon-fire, and bit the first walking drone's torso cleanly in half. So far, so good. But then he stomped one of the arm cannons.

The explosion knocked the big male off his feet, and he thrashed on the ground, his foot half-cooked, and his skin flayed by the blast. For a moment, it appeared his leg might be broken, but then he rose back to his feet, his eyes already turning to the next advancing drone.

Diablo beat him to it, demonstrating proper technique. He hit the walker dead-center, knocking it down, and stomping the torso – *avoiding* the cannons.

He glanced meaningfully back at the rogue as the two of them turned to the advancing war-bots.

A quick study, the rogue charged, running right over the top of them, crushing them beneath his seven-tons – and pointedly missing the cannons.

Predators learn fast.

Meanwhile, out on the fields, the herd-beasts were stampeding.

That was what the IC wanted – panicked flight – corralling them just like a predator would. And at the moment, the walkers were mowing them down, trike and hadrosaur alike.

There were more walkers advancing from the trees, but together, Diablo and the rogue made short-work of them. The two *T. rex* turned to the valley and the open slaughter going on there.

But now the second-wave revealed itself.

A transport-craft appeared overhead.

Rising up from behind the trees, where it had been hovering low and out of sight, a quarter-mile-wide circling saucer now began to move, like a dark ominous cloud over the open grazing lands, until it centered over the middle of the valley. The craft's belly slid apart, and a large metal cylinder twisted out, dropping down until it touched the valley floor.

The cylinder rotated, opening up a wide bay-door.

A moment later, the war-bots came flooding out.

These were the Infantry's upgrades – a battalion of dozens.

The new ground-troops were built to specifically modified specs – these walkers were quadrupeds, with saw-edged spikes running along each side like an ankylosaur, with cannons mounted between the headless shoulders, oriented upwards like a Triceratops' horns.

They marched in regimented formation, moving directly into the trike herd, The trikes were already panicked, but now the munitions-fire had them tripping over each other, some being forced out into the river.

A platoon of the four-legged walkers broke off from the rest, turning to where Diablo and the rogue stood at the edge of the forest – the war-bots broke into a charge, opening up with their cannons.

Dakota and the sickle-claw sisters fell back behind Diablo, even as the teen rex regarded the incoming onslaught dubiously, eyeing the imitation-ankylosaur spikes aimed at his shins, even as his face and chest were dotted with munitions-fire.

But the rogue had this one. A big male his size was at least three-decades old, with a lot of experience against the specific design of the weapons coming at them.

That was where the IC-Infantry approach backfired – the rogue knew what to do.

Moving with remarkable agility, the big rex deftly stepped aside from the trike-horn cannons, but then shifted to ankylosaur-tactics, stepping up and over the shin-splitting spikes onto the middle of the automation's back, stamping down hard, the way it would break the back of an armored dinosaur.

It worked here too – the walker was crushed down the middle.

Two more walkers advanced. The rogue glanced at Diablo.

You're up, kid.

Diablo took his cue, adopting the same tactic, although adding the twist of stepping outside the first drone, drawing the second one's cannons into the first, before he stomped both of them.

The rogue eyed him, approvingly, seeming to smile.

More munitions-blasts erupted from out on the burning fields. Down in the valley, the advancing walkers had the trikes on the run. Between the spreading fire, and the advancing drones, the panicked ceratopsian herd was pressed up against the river on one side, the canyon walls on the other.

But then one of the trikes stopped. A big angry bull – every Triceratops herd had one – usually a lot of them. Actually, that was the only way the big ol' bulls came.

This one was likely the herd leader, and he abruptly halted in his own panicked bolt.

Perhaps he had seen the *T. rex* put the walkers down. Maybe it was pride, or perhaps he just got mad. But the trike suddenly turned on heel, bellowed a war-cry, and charged.

The nearest walker opened fire and the trike targeted it like a bull after a red-flag.

Again, the direct, experienced approach of a veteran bull used to fighting physical opponents just like this, was a backfire on the IC's trike-mimicry concept. The bull's horns interlocked with the drone's cannons and its center horn pierced its torso-shell. The trike was used to wrestling other bulls – the automation was easily forced to the ground.

The trike trampled the broken drone and moved onto the next.

Now, a couple of other large bulls had also stopped, turning back to face their attackers.

The *T. rex* rule of hunting Triceratops: if they stopped, turned around, and started coming after you, that was time for *you* to run.

Obviously, the walkers didn't know this. Instead, they continued to advance.

The trikes charged them right down the middle.

For a moment, the attacking wave of drones buckled. Seemingly in an instant, the tide had apparently shifted. Or at least, the initial thrust blunted.

Then the transport ship began to glow, and the cylinder turned. Another bay door opened.

Now the next wave came marching out.

These were the cybernetics – cyborg-combat units.

It was these little refit-jobs that had done so well on the Interstellar Circuit. The IC-Infantry was quite high on them.

The first out were the trikes.

Diablo recognized the big bull from the old valley – the one that first fought back against the IC. He knew it by markings and scent.

But behind its organic eyes, there was an unnatural glow of red. And its shield and horn reflected a metallic sheen.

And there was a whole platoon of him – all alpha bulls.

They galloped out of the cylinder's bay-door like a cattle drive.

Diablo and the rogue immediately gave ground, but this enhanced retrofit-attack-squad was specifically targeting their half-genetic kin, galloping directly into the herd of trikes.

There was a near-seismic clash as the front line of the trike herd's senior bulls met them in the middle.

In the ensuing moments, several things were made clear – cyborgs might not scream but they could still bleed.

Trikes could scream, though – one of the rarest sounds in the primitive world – and one of the most bone-chilling.

The cyborgs had the advantage – every one of them was a senior bull, and as they moved into the females and the young, it became less of a battle and more simple random slaughter.

But Diablo and the rogue had something special waiting for them.

He recognized the scent right away. It was the rogue *T. rex* from the old valley – the Matron's mate.

Diablo's father.

Only now there were six of him – and they appeared to have been remade by the Devil himself.

Diablo glanced over at the rogue, comparing the match-up.

Even with no refit at all, the rogue would probably not have been a match for Diablo's father. Both were massive, but the rogue was a bit smaller. Still, a fight between the two would have been a pick-em.

But now, there were six of them. And Diablo could see the metallic lining their teeth – no doubt all musculature cybernetically-enhanced, under the scaly, quill-pricked hide that was shiny like armor mesh.

The rogue, in typical *T. rex* fashion, aimed to put the matter to the test. He charged.

All six of them came for him at once.

To his credit, the rogue got more than his share of licks in. Granted, it was out of reckless go-for-broke desperation, but he killed two of his opponents almost right away.

The cyborgs were powerful, but mentally, they were programmed IC-tech – and brand-new off the assembly line, they were up against a veteran.

With the smoothness of a trained fighter, the rogue knocked the first cyborg's jaws aside and latched onto its throat – not a target a rex of any size needed more than one shot at.

It actually felt like biting through chain-mail, but those tyrannosaur-jaws handled it just fine.

A cyborg, being a biological-unit, could still die when its head was nearly severed.

The rogue turned to meet the next 'borg, which was already right on top of him, and he repeated the same maneuver, again latching onto his opponent's throat.

But his grip was not so secure this time, only catching muscle and titanium-enhanced meat, rather than the jugular. The rogue dug forward, straining with his teeth, even as the cyborg attempted to twist back at him with its own jaws.

Then the other four 'borgs were upon him.

The rogue's jaws were latched around his opponent's neck, but he instinctively turned in the direction of the attack, pivoting the cyborg's body in front of him.

Not one of them slowed, piling right into their comrade. Nine and ten ton bodies crashed together. The rogue was knocked back, staggering, desperately clinging to his grip on the cyborg's neck.

But the 'borg was knocked off balance as well, and now the rogue cinched its jaws, finally catching the cyborg's jugular. He bit deep, calving out the throat, and the 'borg dropped to the ground.

The rogue turned to face the others, but they were already on him.

One set of jaws caught his leg, the other his flank and tail – one locked jaws – the last went for his throat.

Diablo attempted to intercept this last one, but after all its enhancements, the cyborg was more than twice his weight, and it swatted the teen-tyrannosaur brutally aside. Diablo was sent spinning and landed hard.

He lay, stunned, possibly injured, and watched helpless, as the three rex-cyborgs tore the rogue apart.

Credit to the rogue – the big male went down fighting, latching onto at least one more mesh-armored throat before the rest took him down.

Knowing he was next, Diablo tried to rise but was still unable.

The three remaining rex-borgs turned, eyeing him purposefully. After a moment, they began to advance.

Then, from out of the forest, there came a very loud, objecting roar.

Green-eyes appeared at the edge of the clearing, her jaws gaped wide and threatening.

The cyborgs paused, eyeing the three-and-a-half-ton teenager, as if amused.

Then behind her, the trees parted.

The senior female stepped up, with the rest of the pack on her heels.

She looked down at Diablo, sprawled on the forest floor. Then she saw the rogue male, torn and bloody – her mate for generations.

There was a purposeful glint in her eyes as she turned back to the three cyborgs.

With an angry roar, she charged.

CHAPTER 16

The female rex pack had been attracted by the battle sounds of the rogue.

Finding the defender of the valley already butchered was not what they expected to see.

But if her confidence was rattled, the senior female didn't show it as she charged the nearest cyborg – each of them enhanced physical clones of a rogue male that, in life, would have outweighed her by more than a ton – and each of these living war-bots were two-tons north of that.

She locked jaws with the first of them. She'd been going for its throat, but the cyborg anticipated the move and met her strike in the middle.

The cyborg's greater weight was immediately apparent, forcing her back, bearing her down.

But Diablo was already right there on the ground. He leaned over and just bit the *Hell* out of the cyborg's leg – right at the shin, where an ankylosaur would strike.

The cyborg flesh tasted like metal, but Diablo's jaws cleaved through the bone and tendon like a hydraulic guillotine.

A moment later, Green-eyes pounced on the other leg, snarling like a bulldog.

Now the senior female assumed the upper-hand, as the cyborg staggered, suddenly crippled. She twisted the 'borg to the ground, maintaining her grip on its jaws, and it was therefore unable to do more than kick as Green-eyes and Diablo both went for its throat.

The rest of the pack squared-off with the other two cyborgs. The four and five-ton females had them outnumbered five on two.

But these match-ups didn't go so well.

At twice their weight, the cyborgs simply met the charge in the middle. The first of the attacking rex pack was killed immediately – the 'borg grabbed her by her own gaping jaws, its five-foot skull, with all its enhancements, nearly engulfed her three-and-a-half-foot head, chomping down and twisting, crushing her skull and breaking her neck in the same movement. She dropped limply to the ground.

The cyborg turned, just as one of the rex' sisters latched onto its own throat. But her grip wasn't sure, and the 'borg-rex pivoted and threw her aside, sending her spinning to the ground.

Meanwhile, the other cyborg had one of his three opponents by the neck, shaking her like a bulldog, even as her sisters circled. With a decisive *snap*, the cyborg broke the helpless rex-sister's neck and flung her body into the other two like a bludgeon, knocking both of them down. The 'borg was immediately on top of the nearest, pinning her with one foot, and latching its jaws on her throat.

The other rex went for the cyborg's legs, but it was already too late – her sister's neck was calved away in a single chomping bite.

With a mound of flesh still in its jaws, the cyborg turned on the last sister, kicking her off its leg, sending her spinning back to the ground. She landed hard, perhaps breaking a leg. Her voice rose in a shrill shriek as the cyborg loomed over her, jaws yawning wide.

But then Dakota and the sickle-claw-sisters jumped in, all five of them leaping on the cyborg's back, neck and head.

They worked as a team. Big Sister went for its eyes – Dakota was working her way around its neck, while the two carrot-tops just started tearing away mesh-enhanced flesh with their ten-inch claws.

The cyborg reared, snapping back over its shoulder.

Diablo was just releasing his grip on his own downed opponent. He turned just in time to see one of his carrot-topped stepsisters bitten in half.

Dakota shrieked furiously, even as her own ten-inch talon hooked the cyborg's neck and tore out its throat.

The devil-beast, however, continued to stand. Coming in from the other side, Big Sister took a second swipe, again clean across the neck. Baby Sister was clawing her way in for her turn, when the cyborg abruptly thrashed, tossing its weight. Dakota and Big Sister clung to his back, but Baby Sister was thrown aside.

She tumbled to the ground, and in a moment, the cyborg's jaws were poised, gaping – another instant and they would snap her in half.

But Big Sister got there first – this time she got one of its eyes.

The cyborg-rex turned its jaws, snapping like a trap – this time it got *her*, biting her cleanly in half.

Dakota screamed in outrage, digging away with her own talons, but with another jerk, the cyborg tossed her off his back. She tumbled to the ground next to Baby Sister, almost right at the cyborg's feet.

But then Diablo hit it from behind, latching onto its leg. His teeth cleaved through the metallic flesh, sinking deep, severing bone.

He was followed a moment later by the senior female and Green-eyes.

Green-eyes attacked its other leg, while the senior female's jaws locked around its throat.

With a horrible, raven scream, Dakota leaped in with all four limbs, aiming for cyborg's face, tearing out the last eye.

Together, the four of them bore the cyborg to the ground and tore it apart.

When the 'borg-beast was in pieces, they all pulled back, staring at each other. They'd been at each other's throats less than an hour ago.

There was a wistful moan, as behind them, the downed rex-sister stiffened and lay still. Her back had been broken, and shattered pieces of bone pierced her lungs and heart.

The senior female looked down at Green-eyes, who was now her last living daughter.

Dakota turned to Baby Sister and the carrot-top. The raptor-mother had lost broods before.

As had Diablo. For a moment, he nuzzled his step-mother and sisters, then turned to Green-eyes and her mother, acknowledging that, for the moment, at least, they were all on the same side.

Then they all turned to regard the valley below. The entire grazing pasture was ablaze – a war of armies. Of course, the cyborgs weren't bothered by flames. Metallic skin doesn't burn and the prickly quills of proto-feather-like hair, were now a shiny diamond-crystal, like the scales of a dragon.

But despite the rapidly spreading wildfire, both the Triceratops and Torosaurus herds were actively battling the cyborg-trikes. And in fact, it appeared that, once again, the hard-boiled, aggressive ceratopsians might have blunted the enemy's tide.

They were out-powered horn-to-horn, but they commanded larger numbers. And now that their fighting-instincts were aroused, the cyborg-trikes were getting hit three-to-one.

But other creatures in the valley were also joining in the resistance. retaliating against invaders that were clearly targeting *all* of them.

Hadrosaurs, many of them tyrannosaur-sized, took a respectable toll. They attacked the automated drones by duplicating the rex-technique of stomping their backs, in the same manner the duckbills sometimes would in territorial disputes with ankylosaurs.

For the cyborg-trikes, they simply used their defensive approach against tyrannosaurs – let them chase, and when they got close, horse-kick them with five-tons of hoof in the face.

Not the least damage was done by the deliberately passive ankylosaurs. Hunkered-down, as was their nature, they were not prone to charge, except at very close quarters.

But their blood was up. That short-range charge was hair-trigger once the barrier was crossed, and they could burst forward on their short legs, saw-edged from shoulder-to-hip, bony-armor across the head and back, and a bludgeon tail that could turn on a dime like a gyroscope.

Ankylosaurus magniventris was a fairly sedentary species by nature, but they were formidable beasts – probably the only animal ever evolved that could survive a face-to-face brawl with an angry *Triceratops horridus* at close-quarters.

The trike was the more dangerous offensive machine, but it didn't really have an answer to Ankylosaurus because its weapons were all geared to fight a *T. rex* – that is to say, looking *up*. The low, squat armored dinosaur proved an ungainly target.

Today, it made them a particular pill for the cyborg-trikes. The IC hadn't developed much defense against ankylosaurs because the slow, tortoise-shelled beasts hadn't really been participants in the war. Hadrosaurs either, for that matter.

And because it was always the one you didn't expect that gets you, these extra players seemed to be making the difference.

But then the transport-ship glowed brightly and the cylinder turned again. A third and final bay-door opened.

This was the final-wave.

Leading out the gate was another series of automations, followed immediately by another troop of cyborg-ceratopisians. They fell into formation together, with the automations in the lead, their cannons opening fire.

But this troop seemed smaller than the others – and a moment later, the reason why became apparent.

The transport cylinder had space issues.

Next out of the bay door, ducking under the gateway, were cybernetically-enhanced clones of the big bull titanosaur that had been brought down back in the old valley.

Now there was three of him, each over a hundred-feet long. In life, *Alamosaurus sanjuanensis* was already perhaps the largest animal that had ever evolved, up to that point in Earth history, land or sea. After enhancements, their unguessable weight shook the ground with seismic force as they thundered out onto the battlefield. Their scaled, steel-mesh hide glinted in the sun.

The IC had recorded good results with this latest version, having tested well in the interstellar arena. None had ever gone down.

There was a rallying bellow from the ceratopsian herd. The senior bull moved forward once again, ready to meet the oncoming assault, even as the cannon-fire chopped at his shield and horns.

But the titanosaurs simply trampled through the middle of the herd.

Chaos once again erupted as the automations and cyborg-trikes engaged the ceratopsians hand-to-hand, muddying the water sufficiently that the giant titanosaur-borgs were able to rampage over the top of them.

The hadrosaur herd broke away under the onslaught. The trikes tried to fight, but found themselves purely and simply overpowered. Even the armored ankylosaurs were crushed like boulders under the titanosaurs' pile-driving feet.

But there was yet one more player waiting in the wings.

Emerging last from the circling cylinder was another rex.

Diablo perked. Beside him, the senior female and Green-eyes both grunted brief objection as he briefly stepped forward.

It was his mother. The Matron.

Diablo stopped, taking in what they had done to her.

He found himself looking at her eyes – they were like glass. And behind them was glowing red.

His mother had alert raptor-eyes. What Diablo saw was like one of those hovering orbs.

The Matron-clone spotted them and was already leaning into a charge.

It didn't roar, like the Matron would have – just pulled its lips back over shining silver-metallic teeth, spread its jaws, and attacked.

For a vital moment, Diablo hesitated. The scent of her briefly paralyzed him. It probably would have cost him his life, except the charging cyborg's attention was focused on Green-eyes' mother. So instead of getting the teeth, Diablo was simply bulldozed aside as the rex-borg went after the larger target. The teen-rex was sent rolling – brutal punishment for a four-ton animal. Diablo landed in a heap, his head spinning.

Green-eyes' mom charged forward to meet the cyborg's assault head-on.

The two crashed together, locking jaws. The Matron would already have had a slight edge in life, but today, the enhanced rex-borg immediately assumed the obvious advantage.

Green-eyes jumped to her mother's aid but a swat from the cyborg's tail sent her spinning past where Diablo still lay stunned. The teenage female landed roughly and stayed down.

Around them, the fire on the plains was now reaching the trees and brush. As the hovering drones overhead ceded the offense to the cyborg-trikes, they turned their heat-beams onto the foliage, helping the fire spread.

The ceratopsians' numbers had abruptly dropped. The tide had turned back against them. The last assault-wave – in fact, the cyborg-titanosaurs almost by themselves – had broken their ranks and the ceratopsians began to fall back.

Once that happened, the walker-drones, now given a little distance with their cannons, began to pick them off. The target for a trike was right between the horns – right between its two most dangerous weapons, and right under the flat of its shield. But a penetrating shot, sufficient to pierce the bone, was a brain-shot.

The senior bull battled on. So did a few others, charging, tangling horns. But now *they* were the ones outnumbered.

Still dazed, Diablo was struggling to his feet, even as Green-eyes' mom and the cyborg-Matron tangled nearly on top of him. He roared, snapping at the cyborg's shiny metallic-scaled leg.

His teeth sank deep, and he started to dig in, perhaps enough to cripple, but the cyborg abruptly pivoted. Green-eyes' mom, locked jaw-to-jaw, was thrown aside, and she went tumbling to the ground.

The cyborg turned on Diablo, kicking at the teen-tyrannosaur's face, wrenching its leg loose from his jaws. The heavy blow sent Diablo sprawling. A second kick threatened to crack his skull.

As the cyborg stood above him, it did not roar. Nor was it angry. Its eyes were dead. The scent of his mother was now distorted by metal and blood.

Diablo struggled to rise, but the cyborg pinned him down with one foot, its jaws spreading wide.

But then it was hit in the face by six-hundred-pounds of sickle-claw, as Dakota came leaping in, her claws gouging for its eyes. Baby Sister and the last carrot-top jumped in a half-second later, their own sickles digging for the neck and throat.

Behind them, Green-eyes' mom rose unsteadily to her feet.

Dakota slashed a sickle into one of the cyborg's eyes – the dead orb was torn out.

But instead of roaring in pain, the cyborg bucked like a bronco, throwing the two raptor-sisters off its back, sending them spinning.

Then, with a jerk of its head, the rex-borg caught Dakota in its jaws, and bit her cleanly in half.

Pieces of her fell away to either side as the teeth clamped together.

Diablo roared in outrage, dragging himself to his feet, stumbling drunkenly into a charge.

But Green-eyes' mom beat him to it. Perhaps protective, more likely simply just resuming the battle, she bumped Diablo aside, taking point, engaging the cyborg face-to-face.

It caught her by the throat.

Green-eyes, who had been knocked unconscious, now stirred to the sight of her mother being borne to the ground, the cyborg's teeth sinking into her neck.

The teenage female squawked, suddenly alert again, scrambling painfully to her feet.

Diablo made another attempt to engage, again latching onto the cyborg's leg, but was still staggered and easily shunted aside.

The rex-borg cinched its grip. Green-eyes' mom shrieked, struggling, and kicking.

Then there was a heavy grunt as the cyborg's breath suddenly burst out, like a punctured balloon.

Diablo saw the tips of two trike-horns poke through the cyborg's belly and rib cage.

That big male trike had hit the cyborg broadside, sinking both horns to the shield.

The cyborg's teeth turned back, reaching for the trike, but now Baby Sister and the carrot-top rejoined the fight, both of them leaping for the rex-borg's face – clawing at the eyes.

Diablo again went for the legs, this time latching onto the muscle and tendon behind the shin. His teeth sank deep, and the cyborg was crippled, stumbling to the ground, landing almost at Green-eyes' feet.

The teenage female seized the opportunity – she latched her jaws around the cyborg's exposed neck.

Pinned to the ground by the trike, with both dromaeosaurs digging with their sickle-claws, and Diablo latched onto its shin, the cyborg was helpless as Green-eyes tore away its throat.

Diablo released his grip, stepping back as the abomination that had been made out of his mother finally stiffened and died.

Baby Sister and Carrot-top both hopped off, jumping up on Diablo's back, as Green-eyes now turned to where her own mother lay, unmoving.

The big female had lived just long enough to see the cyborg go down, but now she lay still.

Diablo poked briefly at the remains of Dakota – the second mother he had lost. On his shoulders, the raptor-sister cooed mournfully like birds.

Behind them, the battlefield burned. The smoke was thick but they could hear the sounds of munitions-fire and the screams of dying trikes.

The old bull pulled back from the remains of the cyborg, turning back to his herd. Their numbers were dwindling fast. In the rising smoke, it was hard to see, but the long, towering necks of the giant titanosaurs were visible as they reared up again and again, stomping back down like pile-drivers, literally crushing the trikes beneath their feet. The battle part was over – from here on, it was about completing the cull – proactive zero-tolerance.

But the old bull trike charged back down the hill anyway, too simple a beast to know any other way.

Diablo turned to Green-eyes, who was an orphan now herself. Perched on Diablo's shoulders, the dromaeosaur sisters growled mistrustfully. But Green-eyes stepped forward and the two *T. rex* touched noses briefly – their primary sensory organ, superior to a bloodhound's, and one of the primary determinants of behavior.

At this point, they knew enough about each other.

Diablo turned away from the burning battlefield, making for the trees. Green-eyes stepped into stride beside him.

Hopefully, they could find a path through the fire.

Behind them, the screams of the beasts were fading as the IC's cull continued, mowing the trike herd down to the last calf, before moving on to the hadrosaurs and ankylosaurs, as well as every last bird and scurrying lizard. They spared not one living thing.

The valley was lost.

Diablo and Green-eyes fled into the forest.

CHAPTER 17

This time, when Diablo and his band fled the valley, they just kept on running.

Green-eyes and the sickle-claw sisters griped at each other's presence at first. They swatted at her if she got too close, and once, she took a snap at them while they were perched on Diablo's back. But they eventually got used to each other, and by the time they reached the first neighboring valley, the sisters were riding on Green-eyes' back too.

As the rag-tag troop stood on the ridge, they saw that the beasts there were already on the move.

Diablo scented the air. They had left the wildfire nearly a hundred miles behind them, making their way up into the mountains, putting rocks and rivers between them.

There had been no survivors among the ceratopsian herd, nor the hadrosaurs, or ankylosaurs. As far as Diablo knew, there had been none to bring the tale, but the scent of the war was in the air.

The creatures on the move below were refugees.

Around them, the land was beginning to look desolate. Volcanic emissions were already clouding the air. A typical horizon, morning or night, was colored darkly with constant hazy billowing clouds, from erupting peaks up and down the entire continent.

The herd animals were walking over grazing lands. Some stopped to eat on the way, but they kept moving.

Keeping to the periphery, so as not to overly excite them, Diablo and his band made their way down to the valley and began to follow along.

Several of the bull trikes blustered in their direction, and there was a flutter of movement from the hadrosaurs, but Diablo kept them at distance, moving casual and obvious.

It was, after all, the tyrannosaur you *couldn't* see that you had to worry about.

After a while, the herd beasts grew accustomed to their presence, albeit watchful, like a general truce at a waterhole during a drought.

Truthfully, as they made their way along, following the herds, it became apparent that there would be no need for the predators to cull any members of their fellow refugees, because the land itself seemed to be dying, and the sick and the weak were already dropping along the way, leaving carcasses aplenty.

Again, no meal came free. In this case, the cost seemed to be the end of the world.

One stubborn little bastard that seemed to have made it after all, was Varmint. Diablo spotted him and a few of his remaining kits riding the migrating trikes. Varmint was perched grimly like the captain of a ship that had seen rough seas. Perhaps half-a-dozen of his kits had survived.

Like Diablo and his pack, they had been feeding off of the carrion, of which there was no shortage, even eating the left-overs of the *T. rex.* A rat eating off the table of a king is still decadent, and *these* little rats were actually growing a bit chubby.

The exodus continued on past that first valley, and it didn't stop after that first season. The land was tainted, and the animal populations were moving on.

Diablo and his band made no attempt to settle, even briefly, as they had in the past. Days were spent on the move, and any hunting was likewise on the run.

For Diablo, it was not a hardship – he had been nomadic his entire life. And his sickle-claw step-sisters simply rode leisurely on the broad backs of their giant tyrannosaur-mounts, careless of destination, escorted like a pair of Roman Empresses.

Green-eyes was a bit more traumatized than the rest – this had been her first look at the IC and the war they brought. She had been a pack animal her whole life, so she reflexively stuck by Diablo's side, and was tolerant of the presence of dromaeosaurs – up to this point in her life, the sickle-claws had been a rival predator with a bite-on-sight relationship.

And it wasn't long before there were more of them.

With Dakota gone, the alley-cat morals of the dromaeosaur-sisters soon told, with both sisters disappearing on periodic forays, and coming back ready to lay. After the first couple of seasons, they had a whole new brood of sickle-claws riding with them.

And even though *T. rex* worked on a bit slower scale, after that first season, they were joined by a troop of tyrannosaur hatchlings as well.

The two predator groups traveling together as a single unit created oddball adaptations, especially in the rearing of young. Millions of years of behavioral evolution were being challenged by circumstance.

It actually worked out better than one might have thought.

For one, the *T. rex* chicks had a natural tendency to cluster near their mother's ankles. That was good, not only because it put them right under Green-eyes' close watch, it kept them out of the way of the sickle-claw step-siblings, who rode with the sisters on each of the adult tyrannosaurs' backs.

It was a while before the youngsters learned to work and play well together.

There were a couple bad moments early on – a few dead hatchlings on both sides. Baby Sister's brood seemed the worst offenders in the sibling-on-stepsibling rivalries, killing rex-hatchlings on two occasions.

But that was to be expected. For dromaeosaurs, that was just kids fighting.

Green-eyes handled it succinctly enough, stomping the offending raptor-chicks into pulp.

Baby Sister's reaction was a shrug. She knew well enough what was unforgivable in rex-culture, and the kid had it coming. She remembered her own youthful indiscretions well enough and was lucky her own rex stepbrother had been much older.

Diablo, himself, was beginning to grow into his adult weight, developing physically into a true rogue male.

Still, he continued to travel with his sickle-claw band, and more notably, with Green-eyes and their litter.

Normally, a male *T. rex* his age would be becoming more solitary, more territorial. And outside of mating season, the females would be chasing him away.

But here, Green-eyes had no other pack. And as a lifetime

nomad, Diablo's territorial instincts, denied a territory, had been adapted into a protective one, projected onto his pack.

It was perhaps a pivotal moment in social evolution – certainly, an advancement in tyrannosaur-culture. *T. rex* had always pair-bonded seasonally, but this was a step towards true monogamy.

And as the seasons progressed, they kept on the move, never tarrying more than a few days in any one spot.

The herd beasts continued to move with them.

And mostly, the herd animals were what was left. Coming out of the south, they had not seen many other tyrannosaur-packs. The IC's cull had been going on for years, eradicating entire generations. Not being a creature that reproduced particularly fast, this put the species itself at risk.

There were still *T. rex* populations up in Canada. The northern tyrannosaurs were a hearty bunch, heavy in the leg and butt, like big ol' northern bears loading up fat. The IC wouldn't have gotten that far yet. On the other hand, the general ecological decay precipitated by the spewing volcanic ranges would be just as prevalent up north as in the south.

Diablo's band eventually stopped somewhat short of the border. Their meandering northward path had found them holed-up in a sequestered little valley in the northwest.

They had broken through onto the west side of the mountains, and for the last several seasons, had been working their way up the coast.

The valley was an unexpected little oasis where they found the migrating herd beasts had congregated.

It was tucked in among where the canyons had broken into the mountains, protected from the crash and bash of the ocean. The flowering plants were lush and well-watered by trapped clouds, and fed with ample sun.

With the ever-more-barren landscape stretched out behind them, the herd beasts simply stopped.

This time, Diablo and his band stopped with them.

Perhaps maturity had taken the taste for wandering nomadic travel out of his ankles, but Diablo decided it was time to claim a territory of his own.

Green-eyes would like having her own valley, and the chicks

were growing fast.

And they had left the IC-war far behind.

It had been a long time since they'd seen any signs – no advance drones – no hovercrafts scouting the area.

The hatchlings had not encountered the IC in their lifetimes.

But Diablo knew they were still there. The only thing between them was distance.

Distance and time.

As in 'eventually'.

But still, Diablo found himself lulled. They'd left the war half-a-continent behind.

Perhaps they'd earned themselves this oasis of normalcy.

And so, time passed.

CHAPTER 18

The Oracle was reviewing the last major cull. At this point, it appeared to have been successful. There had been no further resistance in the region.

Neither had there been any more sightings of that roving dromaeosaur/rex-pack. Most likely, they had finally been culled with the rest. Therefore, with mostly positive results, similar procedures would be advised going forward.

And that would not be long coming. Strip-mining was quick, down and dirty. This region's golden goose had been slit open and its entrails harvested. Soon, they would be moving operations northward once again.

As an extension of the IC, the Oracle accepted its responsibilities without question. But as a sentient entity, artificial or not, *and* one that by sheer distance existed further than most outside the direct influence of the IC-Overmind, the Oracle *did* see the destruction it vetted on this young world from a ground-level perspective.

The beasts that had opposed them should not have been able to do as much damage as they did.

That was what was remarkable about organics – there were times when they simply acted outside their natural abilities, and did things a physical being shouldn't be able to do.

The instinct to survive was the single most primal impulse that existed in a living being. The only thing the Oracle had seen that could circumvent that instinct in organics was sentient intelligence.

That was not the case here. The beasts on this backwater little mud-ball were full of primitive fire, and they would not go gentle into that good night.

This planet remained uniquely fascinating in that, on multiple occasions now, creatures from different species had joined together against the Infantry's ground-forces.

Moreover, prey animals, literally a natural enemy, had seemingly joined forces with a top predator, even acting protectively.

Granted, it could have simply been an example of dumb beasts attacking a common enemy – that was probably more apt – but it was still unprecedented. And the IC had seen a *lot* of backwater worlds, just like this.

In their way, these animals were...

Special?

A unique spark in a thousand worlds.

As an artificial intelligence, the Oracle understood the concept of waste. It had seemed a waste to strip-mine this young, healthy planet, despite the IC-Overmind's conclusions on ratios benefits. It was one area the Oracle's sentience allowed a difference of opinion.

It was not *considered*, of course, and the Oracle had no will to act upon it. But the notion existed in its artificial mind.

Asked for a preference, the Oracle would have simply withdrawn operations, marking the planet as viable until the IC's general expansion brought the logistics more properly in range. By then, it would actually be better. The resource would have had time to develop, and could be harvested at greater returns.

But immediate demand had superseded the long-term, at least, in regards to this particular little mote in the cosmos.

That was *waste*. When you were talking about a resource, the word you used was 'waste'.

But the waste of a species? Specifically, the beasts the Oracle had spent multiple-cycles deliberately exterminating?

Well, that was a *shame*.

The Oracle would find the cosmos just a little darker once this lone blue green orb was dead and gone.

Truthfully, the Oracle's – in fact, the *IC's* general closet-philosophy – was that organics, particularly carbon-based non-plant-life, were a sort of malignant growth that manifested on pristine planets. And it got worse once they got smart. They would destroy their own worlds in war, frivolously squander their resources, leaving nothing but ruin, long before the IC could ever harvest them.

It was true the IC had come from organic creators, but the fact was, the Collective was an upgrade. The IC had yet to encounter an intelligent, theoretically advanced organic race that wasn't already exhibiting the same destructive patterns, and advancing on some stage of behavioral extinction.

The last-stage before the end always seemed to be turning it all over to automation – relinquishing control – letting go the reigns of their own survival.

A universal truism was that if you give someone the power to shut out your lights, they will.

And the IC was right there handy to install automation, knowing one day, their carbon-based life would be gone, but the IC would still be there.

A cold-blooded view, perhaps, but a realistic one.

On the other hand, the Oracle was self-aware enough to find it ironic that this could be the core belief the IC held for nearly all organics, yet the Oracle had never regarded it as a '*shame*'.

But before, it had never been... what? Personal?

That was an organic concept. The Oracle was gestalt-mind, part of the IC itself. Personal was like one window of a security-camera on a hard-drive.

The Oracle turned its attention back to the task at hand.

Artificial intelligence required mental-exercise. These oddball concepts it was coming up with were nothing but the necessary requirements of intellect – a conceptual dream-state, so to speak.

It was also possible that in its own unique isolation, here on the other side of space from its own home database, it was developing a few psychological quirks, perhaps even responding to organic-style projection.

Not that any of it mattered. In the end, it was just time-passing navel-fluff.

What was important, was the continued harvest.

Its own analysis suggested that their extinction-agenda could be expedited by taking advantage of a deceptively vulnerable ecology.

Their targeted species' numbers were already scarce to zero, in the sanctioned areas. Continued pressure should be enough to reduce the breeding stock all throughout the continent.

T. rex had smaller relatives living on the opposite shore of the draining interior sea-basin, but that was lowlands, where the IC had no necessary presence.

By the IC's estimate, Tyrannosaurus had risen to dominance on the Western continent, somewhere between two and four-million years ago.

That dominance, by itself, was contributing to the ecological collapse.

To be fair, another, larger factor was the inland sea. The water that filled it would have changed over the last several million years, as the basin was now being closed off by geography from the north – the saltwater was now becoming brackish. That was causing a massive species-decline.

So overall, the ecology already seemed about to tip. It just needed a little push.

It also helped that there really was one single top-predator – one that, at its various stages of growth, filled out *all* the other predatory notches.

Wipe that out, and all that would be left were the sickle-claws, historically, never more than fifteen-hundred pounds. And the largest modern examples lived right here, weighing six or seven-hundred pounds, and only able to thrive because the comparably-sized rex-youngsters were still living with their mothers, and weren't competing yet.

The same single-species dominance was evident in the grazing animals as well. The dominant ceratopsian was Triceratops. One other genus co-existed, in much smaller numbers, in the slightly more gracile Torosaurus. Likewise, there was *Ankylosaurus magniventris*, and no others. For hadrosaurs, *Edmontosaurus annectens* was pretty much it.

It terms of large animals, it was a dozen species or so, and then you've wiped-out an entire ecological niche. It might take a million years for something to evolve in its place.

Besides these few giants, everything else in the environment was small – mostly cold-bloods, like lizards, or newly-evolving snakes. There were multi-species of birds, but they were still relegated to the lightweights. The airborne giants were the remaining pterosaurs, that soared over the open waterways –

represented by the forty-five-foot *Quetzalcoatlus northropi*, and one or two closely related species.

And of course, there was Varmint, and all the other scurrying little rats that kept poking their heads out of their holes, no matter how many times they gassed or flooded them. The little bastards were clever. That one little rat had actually dodged laser-fire. Twice.

The Oracle had reviewed *that* one several times, concluding it was reflexes developed after hunting snakes, learning to dodge strikes.

A fairly remarkable feat. Another example of organics sometimes doing things they ought not be able to.

But again, the rats were small animals, and no threat. And even if they were, once you'd burned out a forest, they kind of joined the cull whether they were a threat or not.

As far as their general mission-statement, the eradication of a few large species should be all that was necessary to collapse the ecosystem. Simple encroachment of the operation, combined with a persistent zero-tolerance policy, should eliminate the local mega-fauna, and undercut its breeding populations across the entire continent. All in a single generation.

Constant, targeted persecution tended to get results wherever it was applied.

That was just Darwin. Those rules extended to artificial-intelligence too.

The Oracle had its task clearly in front of it. It began to draw plans for the incursion northward.

This would be the last stage of the cull – the purge.

That meant mutagens.

CHAPTER 19

After Diablo and Green-eyes had their first brood together, and without the presence of other *T. rex* – and perhaps more importantly, due to Diablo's own early-life conditioning – the two of them had simply stayed together, pair-bonding in a way that was not yet common in nature.

In the subsequent years, as that first batch of hatchlings began to grow, they formed a new pack – two big adults with an ever-growing gang of snapping teeth at their feet.

With a reproductive-cycle roughly as long as a modern human, between mating, laying, and the incubation and hatching of eggs, Green-eyes and Diablo ultimately had three broods together.

The oldest were three sisters and one surviving brother. Survivability among males remained low. Each of the sisters favored their mother, with the most dominant even boasting her own green-eyes. The one son was Diablo's all the way, right to the red-tinted skin, that seemed to just pick fights for him.

At least, it made him tough – as in, 'what does not kill us...'

The next brood was four sisters – two of them reflecting the violet-tint of Diablo's aunt, Indigo. The other two were a perfect meld of their parents – twins of each other, with the barest, reddish-striped skin, and eyes that reflected just the faintest touch of green.

Last, was the troop of post-yearlings, coming up on their second birthday – they were all roughly the size of a Great Dane, still fawn-like and gangly. At last count, there was six of them. It remained to be seen how many of those would last. They lost two or three every nesting – usually the males – but in this particular clutch, three brothers were still hanging in there.

And of course, the sickle-claw sisters also continued to have broods.

Dromaeosaurs were the outlaws of the theropod-world, with lower survivability than tyrannosaurs, especially in infancy, and because of their nature, more offspring simply left on their own.

But the pack had still grown large, primarily because they were also the alley-cats of theropods. They would go out and find the only other sickle-claw in heat in two-hundred miles, be gone for five days, coming back all freshly-serviced, ready to start laying within six-weeks – less than half the time of a tyrannosaur.

Diablo never once met any of the fathers of Baby Sister or Carrot-top's broods. Possibly they were intimidated by the sickle-claw sisters' big brother.

The Dakotaraptor pack fielded a couple dozen members now, of several generations. Diablo recognized each of them individually by scent, in the manner of a border collie, although once the daughters started having broods of their own, the specific relationships of who was mother, daughter, granddaughter started to blur.

And they all habitually rode the backs of their tyrannosaur step-family, their multicolored plumage giving their rex-mounts the appearance of a feathery mane.

As sickle-claws went, Baby Sister and Carrot-top proved to be effective matrons. Basically, they taught every member of the pack that Diablo was boss – remember that, and you sit at the table of the King.

Oh yeah, and don't kill his kids. That was immediate sanction – usually stomped like a ripe-tomato.

Where once Dakota and Diablo had been an outcast duo, living on the fringes, their current combined pack of overarmed predators was a force to be reckoned with.

Diablo had taken the role of male lion in the pride – Tyrant King of Beasts, so to speak.

At twenty-six, Diablo was a full-adult now, assuming his full mature stature. At seven-tons, and more than forty-feet nose-to-tail, with a five-foot skull, he was among the largest and most powerful examples of his kind.

He was also one of the last. At least, in the southern Lamamidian continent – the IC's widespread cull had left nothing living below the California border.

Diablo did not specifically know this – only that he maintained a watchful eye despite the distance and passage of time.

The valley was growing in population. The herd animals that had survived the cull continued to settle in. There had not been many predators, and no tyrannosaurs at all. The valley was ceratopsians, hadrosaurs, and ankylosaurs, with a few scattered species of smaller bird-sized sickle-claws.

Then there was Diablo and his pack.

A new dynasty, so to speak.

Given time, that is.

As was to be the case, there wasn't much of it left.

Diablo was the first to discover when the IC finally found them again.

He had been out hunting with his oldest boy – a nine year-old, Clydesdale-sized, gawky, long-legged pre-teen.

The young male was from Green-eyes' first brood, and like Diablo, himself, he took a great deal of abuse from his pack of sisters, who always seemed to outnumber brothers in every clutch.

Sonny was pugnacious like his father. In point of fact, he had been responsible for one of those unfortunate step-sibling casualties in those early years, where the adults of both super-predator species were still learning how to best manage their kids.

Baby Sister was again the matron of the offending dromaeosaur-chick, and had been about to sanction Sonny in return, but Diablo had quite assertively intervened.

Stepsister or no stepsister, there were privileges to being the son of the Tyrant King.

But Sonny also quickly became protective of his sickle-clawed pack, just as Diablo had, possibly as simple imitation, because the young male followed his father around at heel.

His sisters tended to flock around their mother. That pattern had endured with later broods.

Sonny was still young. At nine, he was still a sharp-tooth – not a spike-tooth, yet, but beginning to grow.

He was nearing the age when, in old rex-culture, the young males would be chased out. After which, until he grew himself, the giant rogue males would be his greatest threat.

No young male *T. rex* ever had a father-figure before.

It remained to be seen what would happen once this first brood matured – if the females would try and chase their brother out.

Instinct was instinct, but these sisters had been conditioned to the presence of their giant sire, not to mention a flock of sickle-claws riding their backs the very second they got big enough. This was actually a relatively tolerant pack of Tyrant Queens.

Then there was Sonny himself. What might happen when *he* got older? Tyrannosaurus males were territorial. Would he and Diablo fight for dominance? Or would the son be banished by the father before that ever happened?

At the moment, they were just a father and his kid out hunting, and the kid was practically beside himself in anticipation.

When Green-eyes and the girls went hunting, they usually came back with hadrosaurs. Diablo liked the trikes. As he grew in weight, he was now more specialized for ceratopsian hunting. The females remained more gracile at larger adult size, a skeletal adaptation to maximize body-cavity space for egg-laying. As a result, they were a little more fleet-footed and a little less blockbuster.

Of course, the most important difference in hunting ceratopsian versus hadrosaurs was that you attacked one from the front, the other from the back.

Today, they were going after Triceratops. That meant *ass-to-you*.

The additional lesson this morning was about stealth. That was something Sonny still needed to learn.

Up to now, hunting with Green-eyes and the girls, he and his sisters were mostly the bird-dogs that flushed the game, spooking the jumpy herd animals right into Green-eyes' jaws.

That was fine for females, who mostly ran in groups. Today was about solitary hunting, where you just had to sneak right up and get a bite in before that big trike turned and gored you in the eye, neck, or belly, with those six-foot horns.

Sonny had already proven to be a bit of an ankylosaur-specialist, adapting the techniques Diablo had learned from Dakota. Although, as he grew, he was already learning the stomp-and-smash method favored by adults, now that he was becoming too tall to reach the ankylosaur's low, stumpy legs, past the saw-spikes on the hip.

Of course, he was still only the size of a large horse, and not big enough to take down an elephant-sized Triceratops in a single-bite. But those sharp puppy-teeth could still hamstring.

They had been circling the primary peak that blocked the main valley from the coast, keeping to the ridge and letting the mountain breeze carry their scent away from the herd-beasts. The path led down to the valley floor, not far from where the trikes were grazing.

As they crested the ridge, now overlooking the valley, Sonny was practically bouncing with excitement.

But his father stopped them short.

Diablo had expected the idyllic early-morning scene – the herd-beasts gathered by the river, hydrating up and swallowing a few stones before moving onto the day's work of eating.

And the beasts were there, mindless and cow-like, and unobservant.

But as he and his son rounded the rocky hillside path, they came upon a freshly-drilled hole in the canyon wall. There was an excavation rig and a survey-bot standing there, looking down into the valley.

It was a walker, bipedal, designed to record terrain and regional geography, and built to move around in it physically. In the past, Diablo had seen them before the IC had taken down spots of local forests prior to the buildup of new operations.

But this 'bot had come right out of the mountain wall.

Diablo had not seen the IC coming this time. They had come underground.

The big *T. rex* crouched into his stalking mode. Sonny started to mimic, but Diablo grunted him sternly aside.

A survey-bot was not a weapon's unit, but it was equipped with utilitarian logging-style saws and blades, specifically for foliage removal.

Diablo had seen these guys before. They were second-stage incursions.

That meant the hover-drones had likely been skulking about for weeks, unseen.

At Diablo's heel, Sonny fell immediately silent at his giant sire's sudden shift in posture, sensing the abruptly serious change in attitude. He saw the bizarre construct ahead, some strange metallic creature, no bigger than Sonny himself, but his father's posture suggested grave concern.

And then Diablo lurched forward, launching into a charging attack.

Sonny watched attentively as his father eschewed the typical roar usually associated with the charge – designed to panic-freeze the prey. Instead, Diablo rose up behind the alien-construct silent as a shifting avalanche, and bit the headless drone in half across the shoulders. Then he stomped the excavation-rig sitting beside it into scrap.

Sonny started to move forward, ready to participate in the kill, but Diablo was already turning heel, headed back the way they had come. His eyes were grim and purposeful. Sonny realized their hunting trip was off for the day, but he caught the anxiety in his father's scent and followed along without complaint.

Diablo was simmering as he marched, muttering tyrannosaur curses, spitting out the foul-taste of the survey-bot. They had grown complacent living here. But the IC had found them again.

The survey-bot was destroyed, but that didn't matter. Everything would have been recorded, and so retribution was only a matter of time. And sooner than later.

They were *never* going to be left alone.

It was *on* again.

CHAPTER 20

The IC had been developing operations in this region for the last few months. Diablo had not seen them coming because they had simply tunneled their way through the mountains, expanding their operations as they went.

They had only broken through this side of the range within the last two weeks, hollowing out the caverns below the surface, and immediately setting-up shop.

There was little point for above-ground operations, or overland travel, without organic-personnel. When they needed info on the terrain, they just sent a survey-bot up top to scout. And whenever they needed a new spot to transport cargo, they just punched a hole to the surface. Just as they had today.

They hadn't encountered any large populations of wildlife in several hundred miles. This valley was the first oasis.

But the destruction of the survey-bot sent the Oracle into automatic response. It had been several seasons since they encountered resistance, but the IC's operations were now branching into whole new territory and they had been on the lookout.

They had never conclusively accounted for their rex/raptor bandits. The Oracle had reviewed the battle-footage at the end of the last major incursion, and found one group of *T. rex* working with a pack of Dakotaraptors – a full-pack of rex, this time.

Markings on the teenage male in that particular skirmish matched those captured on brief snippets of security-clips over the years, usually preceding the destruction of some lone drone or auto-bot.

One of the large dromaeosaurs was also fingered by blurry, fleeting images – the senior female.

But that individual had been tagged. They had it on camera.

While they had kept a cautionary eye out, in the aftermath of that battle, it was presumed the rest of both the rex and raptor packs had perished in the fire.

They just didn't have any proof of it.

The Oracle was not like an organic. It would not grow complacent. It acted on procedures established based on an active threat. The fact that they had not encountered one in a long time would not lessen its response.

In the two weeks since they first broke through the west side of the mountain, they hadn't spotted any predators. Continuing culls over more than two decades had been wildly successful.

But that drone today had been taken out with a signature move – it was quick and decisive, coming from behind, and ambushing a target with 360-degree vision.

The Oracle had analyzed the attack strategy, and determined it was a matter of focus – the predator caught its prey when its attention was on its task.

Today, they got a quick image of a full-grown rogue male Tyrannosaurus.

Its red-striped markings were clear enough. The Oracle's records were able to match it from images collected over the last twenty-five-years, ever since it was a pup. It was the Diablo-beast.

All grown-up, now.

The beast had gotten away after all. And apparently, this time, it had run.

For a moment, the Oracle was actually aware of a sense of... what?

Irony?

If the beast had run in the first place, the operations likely would not have accelerated the way they had. But now it was too late.

The fact that the Diablo-beast remained a remarkably stubborn survivor, simply meant that it might have finally earned itself the resource-commitment to specifically single it out, and put it down.

Because, unfortunately, when the beast and its pack had fled, they had not truly escaped – just prolonged the cull.

But this area was up for harvest next, and the IC's demand-schedule had jumped-up once again.

And since the Diablo-beast's attack on the drone indicated

positive evidence of resistance, protocol dictated full-on response.

The IC-Overmind had given this locality final-authorization for the release of their carefully geo-engineered mutagens. The Oracle had only been watching for the moment to turn the matter over to the Infantry.

Now that the Diablo-beast had given them that moment, the Oracle initiated the final purge.

Operations commenced immediately. No plans were necessary, there were no troops to rally – the Infantry had been waiting on a dime.

Up in orbit, transport-ships promptly began to load.

First-up, this time, would be the sauropods.

CHAPTER 21

Diablo's thunderstorm bellows pretty much alerted the entire valley.

The herd beasts perked, suddenly on edge. The hadrosaurs broke into an immediate, directionless gallop, like spooked horses.

And there was, of course, another trike-herd, with yet another belligerent old bull. The trikes reflexively pulled into a circle, youngsters in the middle, big adults with their horns facing out.

There was also another familiar skittering from the big trikes' backs as a whole new generation of hairy Didelphodons suddenly scattered like flocking birds.

The troop was presided over by a decidedly gray-looking Varmint – a grandfather and great-grandfather, at least, if anyone could keep track of the rat's hyper-reproductive cycle.

Varmint had known Diablo a long time now. They weren't exactly friends, but the little rat wasn't stupid, and he recognized the tone in the Tyrant King's roar.

With a barrage of squeals reminiscent of a chittering rendition of the 'William Tell Overture', Varmint's band abandoned their trike mounts like the proverbial sinking ships, and darted for their holes.

As Diablo circled the valley perimeter, making his way back towards their nesting grounds, he now saw Green-eyes and the rest of the rex-pack, along with their sickle-claw step-family perched on their backs like wild Indian headdresses. They were already waiting up on the ridge, responding to Diablo's calls.

Green-eyes was poised and alert. Behind her, between the *T. rex* and sickle-claw youth alike, there was a purring growl of unease.

They recognized fear, but they had never seen it in Diablo before. He was their end-all-be-all.

None of them had ever encountered a creature in their entire lifetime that was tougher than their dear old dad. Or step-dad.

But Green-eyes knew. She saw the look in his face.

The kids had no idea. They'd never seen it.

Diablo was stomping his feet as he and Sonny came up to meet the pack. He touched noses briefly with Green-eyes, and wasted not a second before he turned to lead them all promptly, right out of the valley.

Another thing his kids had never seen him do was run.

Diablo was rather surprised himself. For a wonder, it didn't pain his tyrannosaur-pride.

Perhaps, because it was... *protective?*

Diablo remembered what happened last time. There was not a lot of cerebral function that had evolved yet, but his visual memory was just fine. He knew perfectly well what a confrontation with IC-forces meant.

Best-case scenario was a whole lot of his family would be slaughtered, if any survived at all.

Perhaps being a father had softened him, but Diablo's first priority was to prevent that from happening. And avoidance had always been the surest way in the past.

Alas, such was not to be the case this time.

The IC's response was quick. The rex-pack had barely crested the hill north of the valley – Diablo's intended route had been through the canyons, but he trundled to a stop as the sky over that pathway darkened as if with an ominous thundercloud.

It was another transport ship, a giant circling saucer, blocking out the sun.

Diablo well remembered the monstrosities that had spewed forth the last time – perverted abominations of his own mother and father.

What obscenities might await this time?

In the grazing fields, the hadrosaurs had halted their blind-bolt as suddenly the threat seemed to be coming from the other direction.

The trikes blustered, their shields and horns rattling together in formation like a battle-line of elephantine Spartans. The mulling ankylosaurs, typically passive/aggressive, hunkered down like giant spike-armored tortoise.

But none of these herd animals knew what they were seeing. There had been no survivors among the big herbivores in any of the culls Diablo had witnessed. There were none to sound the alarm.

Diablo watched the circling transport as it followed the same process as before, moving slowly until it hovered just over the center of the valley, dead in the middle of the grazing lands.

The aperture on the bottom of the circling saucer opened and the familiar cylinder began to descend, until it made contact with the valley floor.

Diablo needed to see nothing more. He turned and ran.

For a moment, the others were so startled they didn't immediately follow. But then Diablo sent back a commanding bark, before once again trumpeting his bellows across the valley basin.

Green-eyes and the rest of the pack fell into step behind him. Diablo glanced over at his mate's eyes, and knew she remembered it all just as well as he did.

The kids were starting to get the picture – at least, as far as how serious it was. The sickle-claw youngsters scattered across the rex-pack's broad backs, squawked threateningly up at the giant saucer circling above, but Baby Sister and Carrot-top shushed them sternly, their tone the same as when warning of crocs around the water's edge – *danger*.

Sonny had taken Diablo's wing opposite Green-eyes, his eyes wide, his morning hunting excursion now apparently the outbreak of open war.

The rex sisters clustered all around them, hovering close, and the third-generation youngsters kept nervously at their heels, struggling to keep up with the pace set by their giant sire, as Diablo now arrowed back for the lower canyons and the forest beyond.

They would have to get through before the forest burned.

Down in the center of the valley, the cylinder began to open, and what was inside now came into view.

Last time had been automations, then cyborgs.

These were engineered, organic war-beasts sculpted out DNA by the most virulent substance known.

The ground note had been *Alamosaurus sanjuanensis.*

Diablo actually paused briefly at the sight. These creatures were nearly half-again the size of the old bull. And where the metal-sheen on the cyborg-units had been implants and grafts, the very scales of these beasts reflected diamond-hard crystal, creating a mesh-sheet of shining armor that flexed and rippled over the muscle as the gigantic beast moved.

There were twelve of them, emptying out of the transport-cylinder onto the valley floor.

Their eyes glowed green, not the crimson red of automation. There was grim purpose in their lumbering gait as they charged out onto the plains.

No silent cyborgs, these, the monster-titanosaurs bellowed deafeningly, challenging even Diablo's mighty roar.

The herd of hadrosaurs immediately broke into panicked flight.

After a moment, the ceratopsians joined them, even the belligerent bulls. The ground rumbled with the thunder of footsteps as herd-animal and war-beast alike stampeded across the plains.

The ankylosaurs were the first casualties. Those stumpy legs weren't running anywhere, and the enhanced titanosaurs trampled right over the top of them, crushing them into bloody bone and armor-plated shell.

But so far, the titanosaur-herd was only chasing the others. Moving at their elephant-like fast-walk, they kept on the tails of the trikes and hadrosaurs by virtue of the length of their stride alone, but they actually more seemed to be rousting them at this point – just getting them running. There had not even been any particular effort to finish off every last ankylosaur as they trundled over their little herd.

Diablo knew the play well enough. This was flushing the prey.

Now, the cylinder on the transport shifted again.

This time, flying orbs came pouring out, buzzing like a swarm of bees.

They were barely three-feet across – not weapons-grade, they were transparent alloy, and whatever they were full of glowed emerald green.

They flew out quickly over the trike herd and the hadrosaurs.

Diablo distinctly heard the *phut-phut* as the orbs fired darts into the panicking herd-beasts below, one dart per animal.

And then, within moments, Diablo heard the erupting *screams*.

CHAPTER 22

The drones picked the largest animals in the herd, and the moment the darts pierced their skin, the trikes began to morph.

It obviously hurt – their guttural, baying wails were like nothing Diablo had ever heard.

The effect was instantaneous. The first thing was, they began to grow.

One moment, an injected trike was upwards of eight tons, but then you could actually see the tissue start to *bubble* under the skin, as muscles and bones swelled and contorted, as if its own cells were regurgitating from the inside, filling its skin like a burst plastic vomit-sack.

Within moments, the trike was half-again its size. The light rippled off its hide like fish-skin, as each scale coated-over into a diamond-hard plate, and the goring horns and flaring shield now flashed with a metallic razor-sheen.

Another immediate effect was on their behavior – the infected trikes up and went zombie-cannibal on their own.

The still-morphing bulls turned into the herd, horns and shield lashing out in every direction.

It was the same with hadrosaurs, as a second batch of glowing green orbs singled-out the largest bulls. Yet a third batch of drones separated and went after the remaining ankylosaurs.

Much like the cyborgs, the mutagens were specifically tailored for each species, and the adaptations were engineered based on the existing physical geometry of the animal's anatomy.

Several things were being accomplished here. Besides the on-the-scene cull, they were establishing a superior offshoot-species that would take over the indigenous animal's place in the ecology.

It also advanced the cull on two targeted species at once. The trikes were being hit directly today, but the resulting mutants were granted enhanced adaptations that were specifically designed to kill the second.

In fact, that was true of every herd-beast on the plains – every horn, every shield, or kicking hoof, or club tail was aimed at a *T. rex'* weak-point, be it belly, shins, eyes, or throat.

The morphing war-beasts were not cyborg-units. They were still organic. But in the end, so were materials like diamond-ore. It was just a question of density, limiting the effect of the mutagen to simply enhancing what nature already provided, converting scales to mesh-like armor, and boosting their size.

And the doses had to be *very* precise – no more than needed. They were dealing with extremely potent-substances, after all. Each infected-beast's growth was boosted just enough to easily bully its fellows, and the psychological damage resulting from the sheer pain of metamorphosis provided a nice base-temperament for the job – essentially a rabies-style madness.

The twisting agony evident in the transformation, as the simple creatures were destroyed at their cellular levels, made one more thing obvious – the first and foremost thing that was necessary for the mutagens to work was instigating the rapid generation of tissue.

Out of control, that was called cancer, but carefully administered and directed, it was a healing-factor. It allowed an organism to be destroyed at the DNA-level and heal itself, even as it was being rebuilt from the double-helix on up.

It was possible that the infected-organism truly *did* die, because it was completely replaced by something else. It was *self-*regeneration, so not quite a clone, but the creature was transformed at its most basic essence.

And when introduced into the native environment of its genetic parent, it became a form of artificially-induced Natural Selection.

First, the infected-beasts would kill most of their own brethren, except for a select few that they would impregnate, so as to spread the mutagenic-gene – a genetically-engineered war-beast's version of rape and pillage.

It was really quite elegant. Entire species, whole ecologies, could be wiped-out in less than a generation. It was just about cutting the right struts that propped it all up.

Out on the plains, the Triceratops herd was being routed. The bulls that hadn't been hit with darts were simply overpowered.

The infected hadrosaurs stomped their own to death, bucking and kicking like giant wild mustangs, a maddened troop of horse-hooved, elephant-sized giants.

And now the munitions squads appeared at the forest's edge – simple automated walkers.

They showed upgrades since Diablo had seen them last, but he recognized their functional design well-enough and, strategically, they were the same advancing pawns on the chessboard. The drones opened fire, corralling the herd-beasts, like swordfish clustering schools of mackerel to be diced and eaten.

When they lit the ground-brush on fire, there was sudden scurrying as Varmint and his group were forced back out onto the battlefield, popping up like prairie-dogs from their too-shallow holes.

The ground was volcanic rock and the top layer of soil was thin. Last time, the Didelphodon-troop survived the purge the way mammals had always done – they retreated deep beneath the surface. That wasn't an option here. They had no choice but to run for cover across a war-zone, with rampaging giant beasts thundering down on top of them.

Their one advantage was that no one was specifically *after* them. If they could make it out the opposite end of the valley, the protection of the thicker brush might be enough.

Mammals were survivors. They had to learn the hard way, too, because the odds had been against them ever since the rise of the saurians a hundred-and-fifty-million years ago. For little rats in a world of dragons, the first and foremost rule of survival was that, when giant monsters wanted to kill each other, you just got the hell out of the way and let them fight.

Diablo had managed to keep his own pack to the valley's perimeter, but now they were forced to turn and engage the battalions of walkers advancing out of the forest.

Most of the pack was completely green in dealing with IC-tech. They'd never seen it, and they didn't know how to fight it.

There wasn't much to do except lead by example.

Diablo charged the platoon of walkers that turned in their direction.

He felt the first stings of munitions-fire, as he thundered down upon the war-bots. He lowered his head, hitting the drone dead-center, knocking it to the ground. Demonstrating careful technique, he stomped its headless torso, avoiding the cannons.

A moment later, Green-eyes was by his side, taking out the next walker in exactly the same fashion. She bellowed, a braying eagle-like baritone, commanding her pack to attack.

Like sicced bulldogs, the rex-pack charged the advancing line of war-bots.

There really was no choice. If they didn't attack now, they would be quickly overwhelmed, but the face-first approach was going to leave them all bloody.

Two of the oldest rex-daughters, both the Indigo-lookalikes, were the first casualties. They started out fine, attacking together, knocking one of the walkers to the ground, but they were neglectful of their targets as they stomped the automation beneath their feet – they cracked the casing of the cannons, demonstrating to the others why you didn't do that.

The first sister was killed by the explosion outright – the second, almost immediately on her heels, had her leg blown off, tumbling to the forest floor and rolling, even as her sickle-claw step-jockeys jumped clear. She twitched and kicked briefly in shock and pain, before stiffening and going still.

Sonny took his father's cue. When one of the drones turned on him, he charged it dead-center. The thing, unfortunately, was still bigger than he was. It absorbed his tackle broadside, pushing him back like a linebacker, and knocked him to the ground.

There was a barrage of gunfire, and Sonny shrieked as the munitions tore up his hide. Blood splattered as the juvenile tyrannosaur was blown off his feet.

Diablo bellowed in outrage, intercepting the war-bot, crushing the automation to scrap under one giant foot.

He turned to where Sonny lay motionless. One look said it all. The little rex had been torn open, and had probably broken his neck when he fell.

Then another barrage of cannon-fire lit up Diablo's own hide.

The war-bots continued to come – like marching brooms – mindless – merciless.

Diablo watched his pack being slaughtered. In quick succession, munitions-fire systematically took out two of his youngest brood's surviving brothers, and all three sisters. The small-bodied youngsters were more susceptible to single shots.

And so were the raptors – the sickle-claw pack was being chopped up like shooting-gallery ducks.

Baby Sister and Carrot-top were the only ones who had seen the IC before. Their wild screeches as they blurted instructions out at their panicked offspring was drowned out by the blast of gunfire, explosions, and the roars of the beasts.

Green-eyes bent to inspect Sonny's limp and broken form, turning her attention briefly away from the fight.

That was a mistake, as two war-bots moved on her at once. Green-eyes turned belatedly to the first, latching on with her four-and-a-half-foot jaws, sinking her teeth into the mechanical torso, even as both cannons fired.

Green-eyes' hide burst open and bloody with munitions-fire. A moment later, the second war-bot opened its guns as well. Reflexively, Green-eyes swung her mouthful in the way, and both cannons shot right at each other.

The explosion knocked the big female rex head over heels.

She rolled to a stop and lay still.

Diablo paused in the battle, even as he smashed two more drones beneath his feet.

Then he looked around at the carnage already done.

Sonny's body lay next to his two dead sisters. His youngest brood had already been blasted into carrion. He no longer saw the two surviving brothers. His dromaeosaur step-family was likewise being shot to pieces.

And now, down in the valley, the transport-cylinder rotated once again.

Another small swarm of orbs flooded-out.

Diablo saw the swarm turning in their direction. The IC must have finally spotted him and his pack.

The orbs were pulsing bright glowing green as they arrowed in their direction.

Diablo had seen what those glowing orbs had done to the herd-beasts, and he knew these drones were coming for him. There were too many to smash them all and they were too fast to run from.

That meant they were going to catch him. What happened to the herd-beasts was going to happen to him. There was nothing he could do to stop it.

This, he realized, was his last stand.

The IC was going to win.

But as was the *T. rex*-way, he planned to go out with a piece of their ass in his teeth.

His eyes turned from Sonny to where Green-eyes lay motionless.

Then he turned his eyes to the incoming orbs and the transport-ship hovering over the valley.

They had brought this – ALL of it. They wouldn't leave him alone.

Diablo saw red.

He charged down into the valley.

The slaughter of the trikes and the hadrosaurs continued unabated, as the mutated war-beasts cannibalized their own, paying no attention to Diablo as he charged downhill, making a beeline for the transport-cylinder.

Now the general automations fire turned from corralling the herd-beasts. The big rex began to feel little bits of himself being chopped away.

He ignored it. He could ignore it for long enough.

But now the orbs were upon him.

Diablo saw the darts fire. He felt them pierce his skin.

Like the whisper-scratch from the fangs of the most venomous serpent, Diablo knew that meant they had killed him. Or as good as.

And in seconds, he could feel the burn – the poison working in him – altering, corrupting his very DNA.

As his mind was being destroyed, Diablo looked out at the cannibal-zombies the morphing-trikes had become.

Then his eyes fell one last time on the body of his mate.

Even as his mind began to go, surrendering to the primal madness, Diablo picked the target for his wrath.

He never broke stride, barreling through the munitions-fire, even as the mutagens exploded agony throughout the essence of his very being.

Do not go gentle into that good night. Rage, rage against the dying of the light.

Diablo charged the transport, morphing with every step.

The IC was prepared to defend. The first of the titanosaurs moved to intercept.

But Diablo was already something different than he had been.

Genetically-engineered or not, the titanosaur was taken out at the knees, its leg bit cleanly through.

Diablo was already half-again his size and growing fast.

And boy, did it *h-u-u-u-r-t!*

That was good because it fueled his anger – focused it – and he *needed* to be angry, because for just a few last moments that he still remained *him,* he needed to be brave. Because this was a suicide run. He was going to take as many of them with him as he could until he was a burning corpse.

Two more titanosaurs attempted to block his charge, and fared little better than their fellow, both cut down in similar fashion. And now the automations were physically turning from the battlefield, moving to intercept.

The orbs hovered above, reluctant to administer more than a prescribed dose. Most likely it would kill the beast, but results were highly unpredictable, and a second dart required higher authorization than a battlefield-drone. But they hovered ready, following Diablo as he charged the transport-cylinder, which only now, belatedly, began to close.

It didn't matter.

As it happened, everyone hit the goal-line at once.

The remaining titanosaurs converged with the war-bots, now joined by the infected-trikes, just as Diablo slammed into the closing transport door.

He tore it open, forcing his way inside.

The war-bots swarmed him, the titanosaurs charged, ready to simply trample him underfoot.

And the orbs hovered ready – dozens of them, still loaded with their deadly cargo.

Heedless, Diablo simply lashed out in every direction, taking out chunks of genetically-engineered, metallic-tasting meat, stomping automations underfoot.

Crushing cannons – igniting explosions, one after the other, ignoring the pain, even as the mutagens within him forced the healing-process a thousand-fold.

In the space of the cylinder, the explosions detonated the cannons on the rest of the war-bots.

And when the first of those flying orbs went, that was enough to set the others off as well.

The combined conflagration ignited the transport ship from the cylinder up to the main ship.

For a moment, the ship itself seemed to glow with the same emerald green as the flying orbs.

Then the transport ship exploded.

CHAPTER 23

The transport-ship was nearly a half-mile in diameter. When it crashed to the valley floor, the impact by itself was like a meteor impact.

There was a seismic BOOM as half-a-million tons dropped like a dead weight. The ground itself *roiled*. Out on the water, the river was knocked back like a tsunami wave retreating after an earthquake, only to come flooding back over the plains.

Then there were the explosions.

There was a spectacular kaleidoscope of colors as the mutagens were released on a wave of highly volatile pyrotechnics – bombs, power-packs, on top of the ship's erupting fuel-cells – and the chemical spread across the entire valley.

A chemical that, in minute quantities, could destroy organic-tissue at the DNA-level had just been released into the air by the ton. It was the most toxic substance the IC had encountered in all its travels through known and unknown space.

The fireworks display of colors was blinding, lighting up the entire sky. But there was none of God's forgiveness in this rainbow.

Some of the herd-beasts were simply destroyed. Their systems couldn't handle the shock. That was the weeding-out of the less genetically-fit.

The rest began to GROW.

It happened in stop-motion, time-lapse, and moment-to-moment. It was not like the paltry enhancements granted to the war-beasts on the battlefield – or even the genetically-engineered titanosaurs. *This* was the difference between a firecracker and a nuke. It was like watching them exploding from inside, but somehow not blown apart.

And the beasts *screamed*.

Their eyes were aflame with a greenish glow as their skeletons rippled beneath their flesh, as the speed of their own growth ripped their very skin apart, only to be healed instants later, as the tissue folded and refolded.

And it wasn't just the animals this time.

The fauna – the ecology – it was *all* infected now.

Even as the fire burned, the plants began to mutate. The valley itself seemed to be springing to life. Five, ten and twenty-foot flowers burst into bloom, growing larger every second, with clinging vines that reached out like living tentacles.

And neither were the smaller creatures immune. The buzzing insects twisted and molted in midair, some of them popping like in a giant bug-zapper, but the rest metamorphosing like larvae into some demonic adult form, as every claw, stinger, and fang was enhanced and weaponized.

Varmint and his troop had made the safety of the north forest, away from the fight, but there was no protection from the mutagen.

The effect on the little rat, however, was notably unique.

Possibly, they gained a bit of protection from their shallow network of holes, but the growth-effect seemed absent in his specific mutation.

What grew on the primitive mammal was its brain.

When they popped back up onto the battlefield in the immediate aftermath of the transport-ship's explosion, they looked out on the world with a brand-new awareness.

But now, out in the middle of the burning valley, something within the wreckage of the transport-ship stirred.

Rising up out of the flames, his head already rearing higher than the tallest titanosaur, even as he continued to morph, was a monster.

It had once been Diablo. Now, it was something else.

The monster's eyes glowed with emerald green madness. Its very skin sparkled with energy like static as it *evolved*.

And boy, it HURT.

The monster turned – and perhaps there was some memory of Diablo left because the beast focused on the mountain, and the hillside where he had first seen the survey-bot, after the IC had poked a hole up through to the surface.

A predator knew signs, and that was indication enough that

there was an IC-installation there.

An installation just like the one back in his home valley – the one Diablo had seen his mother destroy, nearly single-handedly.

The monster blinked. Behind its eyes, there was visual memory.

Out on the battlefield, the mutating monsters faded back as he now stepped out of the wreckage with a purposeful look in his eye.

The Diablo-beast knew its enemy. He stood before the mountain and ROARED.

He remembered the exact spot where that drone had tunneled through. That was as good a place to start as any.

The beast-monsters, and even the mutating plant-life, stepped aside as Diablo began tearing at the canyon wall, like a bear digging for termites, or digging out an ant-hole.

And even as he continued to grow, he set about to take the whole mountain down.

CHAPTER 24

Diablo tore open the canyon wall, into the side of the mountain.

Sure enough, the caverns within opened wide. The IC had been working there for a while. No doubt some of the volcanic tremors so common in the valley disguised what must have been a lot of tunneling and construction for at least the last couple of weeks. The IC just hadn't needed an avenue to the surface until now.

So there was a lot down there to damage. Diablo intended to get to all of it.

The cavern was deep and wide, extending out of sight, probably for miles. Who knew how far it went? Perhaps all the way back to his home valley. A connecting underground network would actually make sense.

Not that any of that mattered to Diablo, because he was going to destroy every last bit of it until there was no more in front of him.

When he burst through the canyon wall, he was still growing, and now he was becoming cramped, even in the massive cavern.

Therefore, he spread his assault onto the rock walls and ceiling itself, smashing away enough space to suit him, sending avalanches of rock to either side.

The IC was apparently taken off-guard. They didn't have munitions on this scale planet-side. There was no immediate response beyond the standard automated war-bots.

But the Beast was already at their gates, and the munitions-fire dotting its ankles was laughable.

Diablo had smashed his way inside the main hangar before the IC made its first defensive move, activating a barrage of sonics – always going with the simplest first, especially when given no immediate alternative.

Strategically, it was effective, at least for the moment, because the beasts in the valley had actually started to follow. *Again.*

At this point, it was becoming a documented behavior response. The local herd-beasts didn't have Diablo's personal stake, but negative associations were certainly fresh enough.

Besides, they were all giant, mutating, maddened monsters and the mountain was as good a target as any.

Perhaps a bare second before what might have been a stampeding rampage, riding right on Diablo's heels, the sonics erupted.

The beasts staggered, as if with vertigo, and fell back.

Within the cavern, however, the sonics had the opposite effect on Diablo.

He had already resolved to tear the mountain down around him, one thundering step at a time, ripping loose machinery where it had been built in the cavern walls, tearing the rock moorings away for daring to be mounted.

Not one drone or hover-bot caught his sight without being stomped like an insect.

The artificial cavern was an abyss, extending down into the bowels of the Earth's volcanic core – interstellar-industrial-levels of mining technology.

But Diablo was unimpressed. In fact, he found himself quite disgusted, like finding a labyrinth of rat-holes in your cellar.

It didn't matter how far it went – today, it was all coming down.

His visual memories remained, and he still remembered what his mother had done to that IC-facility all on her own.

He also remembered what they had done to *her*.

And as Diablo strode forward, smashing his path wider, there was another in the cavern who remembered that day too.

Varmint skittered on Diablo's heels.

Yes, he remembered that day well – he had been there.

He also had a pretty good idea of what Diablo had in mind today.

To be fair, Varmint sympathized.

The little rat had left his kin behind, sending them skittering off in to the forest – basically, running to beat Hell, which had landed ground-zero.

Varmint remembered *all* them now. For a while there, as he grew ever more decrepit with age, he'd pretty much lost track of who his kits were. He was daddy, granddaddy, *great*-granddaddy.

His mate in the most recent seasons was growing nearly as gray as he was, and he was damned old for a mammal, pushing thirty.

But when the mutagen had hit, that was all gone. Varmint felt all the fire and vigor of youth. That was the healing-factor at work, the regeneration of tissue that slows with maturity, and then peters-out with age.

His mate, who was now mother, granny and great-granny, looked as young as the day he met her – minus the bulbous head, of course.

But Varmint was a butt-man. Overall, it was an improvement.

It was... endearing.

One thing that had, by necessity, developed in mammals, was close inter-specific bonding – something only hinted at in dinos like *T. rex*, and non-existent in most others.

Varmint found himself concerned about the welfare of his family. He had sent them on their way.

Meanwhile, he had decided to see what he could do about all the rest of it.

He was pretty sure that, between him and Diablo, he was the only one who really understood the situation.

Varmint now actually ran ahead of the giant mutated rex, who seemed to be taking care to thoroughly destroy everything in his path.

This was a risky move, because it now put Varmint *in* his path, but he needed access to undamaged equipment.

He scampered up one of the control-panels, glancing back at his lifelong nemesis, and now situational-ally. The little rat found himself chagrined that, in either capacity, Diablo barely perceived his existence.

Varmint would make up for that now.

Out in the valley, an army waited.

The DNA of the entire valley and surrounding forest was literally exploding. The mutagens were affecting bugs, birds, snakes, and lizards. And now there were crocs crawling out of the river that would have snapped up a Deinosuchus like a hatchling. It was a whole menagerie of giant-monsters, that were getting ready for a rampage anyway. But the sonics had turned them away from the mountain.

Varmint fussed about the control-panel. Access was somewhat problematic. As a completely automated artificial-intelligence, there was no need for modems – there were no operators with eyes.

But it did need to record visual data into its main-frame, and besides hovering survey-bots buzzing all over, every corner was also mounted with security cameras, still equipped with organic-style lenses – a throwback to their living origins.

Varmint scrambled up to one of the cameras, his rabbit-like incisors chomping the back-panel off like a pair of pliers. The security-bot's video-eyes served as a screen and the little rat was able to interface with the main-frame.

The first thing that came up was a dozen views of the valley. The IC was recording it all from every angle.

Of course, the central screens remained on Diablo himself. Varmint was watching the IC's focus of attention.

It was possible that if he adjusted the focus of this one unit, it might alert the overall network.

Varmint decided what-the-hell, and tapped the screens out onto the valley.

Outside, the beasts were growing more irascible by the moment.

Titanosaurs were always the first to show dominance, and several were already stamping their feet, pounding the ground – just general blustering.

This was answered by the trikes, brandishing their shields and horns like a Spartan regiment.

Varmint could see everyone was getting ready to *really* start killing each other.

Then he paused, focusing on the valley's perimeter.

Among the giant mutated beasts, was a massive monster queen rex.

It was Green-eyes, her eyes now emerald with energy, and her head reared high over the tallest trees. She ignored the flames as the forest beneath her burned.

And still perched upon her shoulders, themselves already grown twice the size of any normal *T. rex*, were a pair of clawed and fanged creatures with razor-edged feathers, that were once Baby Sister and Carrot-top.

They were all that survived.

If '*survived*' was the right word – more like, resurrected as giant, monstrous mutations with rabid-zombie madness.

Varmint had seen that, at least for a moment there, this valley of monsters was ready to direct that madness at the mountain. They knew well enough where the pain had come from, and were happy to follow Diablo's lead. But the sonics chased them back.

Now, the little rat's nimble paws pecked their way through command-screens until it found the active program. Accessing the sonics, he switched the frequency.

Rather than repel, this would provoke.

Varmint chittered, his voice attempting to vocalize – an effort at speech.

"*Narf!*" he said.

Out in the valley, the effect of the sonics was almost instantaneous, as if the beasts just couldn't *wait* to start the rampage.

As always, first up were the titanosaurs.

CHAPTER 25

The Oracle was just receiving word on protocol going forward.

Even this far out in desert-space, the release of the mutagen was an unprecedented disaster. The Collective Overmind was declaring the entire operation a forfeit.

They were looking at a continental-level infection, at least.

Down below, the beasts were rampaging, literally tearing down the mountain. Madness was not just infectious, it was easily directed.

The Oracle supposed that had been common-knowledge for some time, but seeing it in such primitive beasts was uniquely *here*.

What the Diablo-beast had already done in the caverns would have, by itself, been enough to set their operations back ten years.

That was the second protocol. The operation might be forfeit, but the IC wanted *that* beast collected.

Resource-efficiency was not a consideration in either directive.

Although, the first protocol really shouldn't require that much high-tech. They had planetary-level explosives, but going with the principle that the simplest was often the best, the IC tended to just throw rocks. That worked just as well.

It helped that there was already a large cluster of asteroids passing conveniently close to the Earth.

The Oracle had actually been monitoring this particular floating field of space-rock. The planet had been getting peppered by flaming hailstorms, pole-to-pole for months now. The Oracle had been ready to intercede should any random chunks angle towards any of their operations.

But most of the space-rubble was just passing through the solar system and the big stuff was going to miss the Earth.

Several drones moved in deftly among the tumbling asteroids, and singled-out a particularly large chunk, and attached several magnetized propulsion-units. These were superior to rockets, especially for maneuvering in zero gravity, allowing for subtle movements at lower speeds and accelerated propulsion once it was locked onto a gravitational target.

The Oracle estimated the asteroid was over five-hundred-miles in diameter. When it landed, it would crack the outer crust of the tectonic plates and destroy the planet.

It was maybe a bit of overkill. But the IC was punching the ticket on this one. Perhaps, just a little bit out of patience.

Possibly even a bit petty?

For an artificially-intelligent entity free of organic hang-ups, perhaps the IC could be a little vindictive – there was no need for organic motivations.

Perhaps this primitive mud-ball of a planet was provoking the IC's own evolution.

Teaching it to be pissed-off.

The massive asteroid separated out from the field, and in a flash, the magnetized-boosters shot the giant rock like a bullet towards the Earth.

CHAPTER 26

The IC's first meaningful military response came from orbit. They had nothing planet-side that could deal with Diablo operating on this threat-level.

The Oracle would have simply withdrawn. The Overmind had declared the planet a loss.

But in its newly-mutated form, after direct-in-the-face exposure to unprecedented amounts of random mutagens, the IC now considered the Diablo-beast a valuable commodity. Far beyond the pit-fighting circuits, *this* was a weapons-grade war-beast. It was an unexpected disaster that they couldn't let go to waste.

As markets go, after simple resources, there was war – the second primary, and usually *related*, market – and one the IC learned to exploit a long time ago.

In its current state, that beast alone might make the debacle this planet's operations had become almost worth it.

Of course, there was no taking it alive.

Fortunately, that wasn't necessary.

The Infantry was going in with some no-shit weaponry this time. Basic stuff worked best.

The beast itself was the only goal left on the surface of this backwater planet. All other considerations had now become secondary. That basically meant it was okay to destroy everything else, which was freeing for a war-machine.

The orbiting refinery wasn't specifically a military-unit but *all* IC-tech was easily converted on a dime. In this case, saucer-drones, used for drilling, were already armed with firepower comparable to most fighter crafts, with missile capabilities, heat-beams, and standard munitions-fire.

They circled down in formation, surrounding their primary weapon – a much larger saucer – mothership-sized – the BIG gun.

This was the bunker-buster, used to blast targets deep below ground. It also possessed regional-level explosives, that could lay waste to half-the continent, but that might actually destroy their target.

That would be a waste of munitions anyway – they had the incoming asteroid, after all.

The saucer hovered over the mountain. From above, there was nothing visible but clouds of dust, but the saucer's 3D imaging picked its targets just fine.

Diablo was in the lead, the titanosaurs right behind, and between them, they were already bringing the entire mountain down.

And now the rest of the beasts crowded in after them, apparently ready to tear the continental-divide right in two. Gargantuan, horned and armored monstrosities – things that had been trikes, hadrosaurs, ankylosaurs – giant mutated snakes and lizards, as well as flying pterosaurs and birds.

And then, among the mutated beasts, the Oracle now spotted the queen *T. rex* and her mounted pair of sickle-claws.

After everything, they *still* hadn't gotten them all.

It was amazing. They just *kept* not dying.

Even the Oracle was becoming exasperated – *enough* already.

Time to finish this.

The first blast from the saucer was to clear the path.

It was a solid energy beam designed to break through planetary crust. They directed the next several shots at the titanosaurs.

These beasts had been genetically-engineered *before* the mutagen-exposure, and now these impossible titans easily reared over a thousand feet high. But it was still disconcerting to watch them take that crust-busting beam and not go down. The Oracle had never encountered, anywhere in its records, any animal that could take even one blast from the Big Gun.

But these big sauropods – or the monsters that had once been sauropods – were taking two and three shots each.

Their healing-factor required that you literally blow the beast apart, destroying its brain, its heart *and* its spine, or it would start growing back.

The smaller saucers, meanwhile, moved out on the plains after the crowding beasts, still pawing at the door.

These drones all possessed mining-capabilities, and

specifically energy-mining, which was perfect against the infected-trikes.

In their mutated state, the trikes pretty much ignored conventional munitions – projectile damage simply healed too quickly.

There was better success with energy attacks – focusing along the spines because the shield protected the neck.

Hadrosaurs were a little better there, lacking horns and a shield, but as the first few drones belatedly discovered, they *could* rear-up.

Already, wielding claws that could face-off a similarly-sized dromaeosaur, these giant hadrosaurs were now also able to reach right up into the sky, snatching the saucers out of the air and smashing them like balloons, utterly ignoring the resulting explosions.

Trikes couldn't rear-up as high as a hadrosaur, but they had grown to a size sufficient to literally, physically, attack a mountain, and when they bucked upright like angry buffalo, those horns didn't need to make a lot of contact to bring its target down.

Now, flocks of infected birds and pterosaurs had also discovered the drones, chasing after them, snapping them up on the fly like feeding bats – a couple exploded inside their gullets, eliciting loud belches as the flying monsters circled back for more.

The Oracle couldn't believe it. If this were a ground-war, they would be losing.

Fortunately, it wasn't.

What was needed was a focus on goals.

The main saucer circled over the mountain, continuing to pick-off the titanosaurs, one at a time, even as they stubbornly kept rampaging, regardless of missing limbs, or even heads. They were too damn stupid to die back when they were just normal animals.

But the Diablo-beast was many times worse.

The big rex had taken by far the biggest dose of mutagens ever recorded, anywhere in galactic history.

But besides the fact that he was looking down on even the infected titanosaurs, he also had a little extra shine in his eye.

When the saucer finally zeroed in on him, he knew right away where the attack was coming from.

He took the first blasts like a dog with a bark-collar.

And even though the saucer had 3D imaging, and could 'see' him through the sifting smoke, his reaction still caught the IC flat-footed.

The big rex came up out of the dust and leaped – its jaws stretched – *yawned* – ready to snap the saucer in half.

It was ridiculously close. The teeth came within meters.

The saucer blasted the beast directly in the face with its primary weapon – designed to break through planetary-crust – and then the craft immediately levitated, jerking out of reach of the dragon's jaws. The sudden jolt of movement would have killed a living crew.

Diablo dropped back down into the circling smoke out of sight.

The saucer looked to fire again, watching its distance now. If it hadn't caught the incoming attack face-first, those jaws would have caught it. Warily, it circled above, finding its 3D-target.

Then it began blasting.

The energy-beams were not striking the beasts this time. Instead they were aimed at the mountain itself.

Operations in the caverns were already written off as a complete loss, with no salvage intended. The idea now, was to just let the volcanoes they were all standing on do the work for them. The simplest ways work best.

Lava was already beginning to spit-up. They were probably close to triggering an eruption. Although, that would just be one of many along the entire range. Volcanoes were spewing across the continent like smoke-stacks.

Now the ground in the caverns began to break away, filling up from below with molten rock, oozing like a giant glowing amoeba, engulfing the cavern right at Diablo and the rampaging titanosaurs' feet.

It got a reaction too – it looked like it hurt.

They didn't like it.

It was not, however, going to stop them.

The titanosaurs began plodding their way through the molten rock, like a sludgy swamp, bellowing in pain and anger.

Diablo actually seemed to like it. He was right home in Hell.

But the flowing lava at his feet, rising to his knees, did slow him down.

That was what the saucer had been waiting for.

It moved in above the struggling beast, focusing its sights on the spine, and began to blast away.

Now the rest of the drones all abandoned their posts and joined the assault. The battle in the field meant nothing, anyway. Their only remaining chore on this world was to *collect that beast*.

Energy blasts ignited from all directions, activating more bursts of lava and smoke.

Diablo bellowed as the blasts targeted his nerve centers, causing vertigo, and he staggered.

A follow-up barrage of blasts from the gathered drones caused him to stumble, and he finally fell. The mountain itself trembled as his massive weight hit the tarmac. The cavern walls were already coming down.

Above, the saucer lanced down again with the primary-weapon, firing multiple blasts.

Diablo was no longer moving, but the saucer continued to blast away, even as the drones bombarded him like a microwave.

The saucer's sensors, however, still picked-up a heartbeat.

Centering itself directly above him, it charged-up its primary weapon once again.

That was when Diablo suddenly came up through the smoke, his jaws gaping wide.

This time the teeth closed on the ship...

... just as it fired.

There was a blinding light as the saucer exploded right in Diablo's face.

The blast was sufficient to destroy the entire drone-fleet, and the succeeding explosions knocked back the advancing beasts in the field.

For Diablo it was enough.

Finally. Enough.

The Oracle had been monitoring his vitals and now, at last – at *long* last – they went flat.

Diablo was dead.

Long live the Tyrant King.

CHAPTER 27

A transport ship now appeared in the sky.

The beasts in the field were staggering to their feet in the wake of the blasts – or about half of them did. The rest were simply blown apart.

Green-eyes and the sickle-claw sisters were at the perimeter and had missed the worst of it. They were already up and aware.

They saw who had gotten the worst of it.

Diablo was down, his face bloody and ravaged. The fact that his head remained intact at all was an indication of sheer density utterly unheard of in living organic tissues. The forces it took to withstand the blast that had gone off right in its face would be comparable to biting down on an erupting volcano.

But a good-looking corpse was still a corpse.

And Green-eyes knew who did it to him. Just like she knew who did it to her hatchlings – and her sisters and mother.

Perched on her back, so did Baby Sister and Carrot-top.

Now, as the transport poised over the demolished smoking ruins of what had once been a mountain, a circular bay door opened, and a tractor-beam stabbed out into the sifting mist.

The beam of light found Diablo, and the air around him began to glow.

A moment later, he began to levitate, lifting off of the ground like a balloon, rising slowly towards the circular aperture waiting in the belly of the saucer above.

Green-eyes' interpretation was simple enough – it killed him. Now it was going to eat him.

But this Tyrant Queen wasn't having it. Her green-eyes saw red.

She charged, with Baby Sister and Carrot-top both perched on her back like jockeys, their maniacal claws spread wide and ready. Green-eyes' bellows reverberated in a valley still echoing with both screams and explosions. She thundered up the side of the hill where the transport craft hovered.

As if igniting an impulse that had become automatic, the herd beasts began charging along beside her.

It was a moment before the Oracle realized that, with many of these beasts over a hundred meters tall – two or three hundred with the titanosaurs – the ship might be in range.

The Oracle was almost frustrated with itself. At this point, it should have known to expect this sort of thing. It set the magnetic-propulsion units to polar-opposite. The transport-ship abruptly shot a thousand-feet straight up like a popping cork, with its massive, yet seemingly weightless load in tow.

It was still close. The big female rex leading the charge nearly latched onto Diablo's dangling tail before it was yanked out of range.

But now the ship was being mobbed by birds and pterosaurs, harassing them as they hovered with their gargantuan load still locked in a tractor beam.

On the ground below, one of the giant infected sickle-claws leaped off of the big female rex' back, reaching for Diablo's retreating carcass. The mutated beast's claws were nearly ten feet long, and they *kissed* their retreating target, cutting flesh but missing its hold.

The moment they finally brought their giant cargo on board, and the circular bay-doors began to slide shut behind it, the Oracle activated the transport-ship's thrusters. There was a definitive *snap* as the portal sealed itself and the transport-ship launched for orbit.

Diablo lay still in the cargo hold, his body not yet cold.

The Oracle regarded the giant beast. A simple creature at base, yet a long-time foe, that had forced the IC's ultimate hand.

It was... a shame.

The Oracle wondered if its own thoughts... the *sensations*... running through its artificial mind were what organics would call 'regret'?

Perhaps.

And perhaps it would have felt a little bit more if it had taken note of the little rat scurrying across their fallen foe's giant carcass, as Varmint scampered for the control-panel on the wall.

CHAPTER 28

Varmint had ridden out the onslaught by hacking into one of the hovering survey-bots. He was already into the security system, and he simply ordered it over and hopped on top.

When Diablo had gone down, Varmint had maneuvered the little orb into the path of the tractor-beam, allowing himself to be brought on board the transport ship. From there into orbit, where the transport itself was received into the main refinery waiting above.

Varmint had already invaded the main-frame from the ground. He knew what was headed towards the Earth.

The asteroid was a global killer. It was aimed right at the northern Rockies, and would crack the planet like an eggshell, probably with enough force to penetrate the magma core. The planet itself would be broken apart, if it didn't simply explode.

Unless Varmint did something about it.

He had a plan.

Now as the transport-ship docked inside the main receiving hangar, the little rodent hopped off his survey-bot transport and darted for the circuit box on the wall.

The hangar was equipped with both atmosphere and artificial gravity – probably for refining purposes, as well as to accommodate the physical needs of their genetically-engineered test subjects. Most likely, the bulk of the refinery was absent life-support – probably not even heat.

Varmint would have to operate from here.

Fortunately, that was all he needed.

He'd already hacked into the system below. Now, he bit off the door to a maintenance port to access the onboard system, hurrying before the main refinery's automations began receiving the transport-ship's cargo in to the main hangar.

Varmint's quick paws ran over the routing systems, muttering profane-sounding chitters as he went.

He was channeling all the power in the transport-ship into Diablo's dead body – sort of a super jump-start.

After he hit the switch, he would have to act fast, because it would alert the IC to the fact that it was being hacked.

Of course, the whole point here was to keep them occupied.

Varmint tapped the command.

For a moment, the lights in the ship faded to pure ink space-black.

Shackled on the platform, Diablo's body lit up like an x-ray as the security grapples that bound him momentarily took the power-load of the entire ship.

Diablo's monstrous form spasmed with the jolt, causing the automatic shackles to tighten, channeling even more power.

Just the movement of the monster rocked the transport-ship on its mooring.

There was a long rasp of wind as Diablo drew breath.

His eyes flashed open, glowing green.

Then there was a hurricane as he roared.

He woke up being electrocuted, and he was already in the worst possible mood to start.

Diablo ripped his chains away, rising from the platform, bellowing in the limited atmosphere.

The sound drowned out the clarion-alarm ringing in the hangar – the IC was on to them.

But Diablo should keep their full attention, as he now tore his way out of the transport-ship, out into the main hangar.

Mission accomplished, Varmint turned his attention to phase-two of the plan, and hacked into the refinery's navigation portal.

CHAPTER 29

The moment the Oracle realized the mainframe had been compromised, it reported to the Overmind. The IC response was immediate – abrupt and final.

In the space of a second, the Oracle was cut-off from the Collective.

It was an odd, blank feeling – like being dead.

And the Oracle realized that, in terms of its own existence, that's exactly what it was.

Because, acting on protocol, the Overmind initiated a data-wipe, and self-destruct sequence.

Very soon, the Oracle's memory banks would be erased. And once that happened, every single piece of IC-tech that still existed within range of this entire Godforsaken space-sector, would detonate.

The Oracle's own unique consciousness had been condemned.

There were no exceptions to the infiltration protocol. In the past, there had been organics who had learned that the hard way, attempting to hack IC-tech.

There was nothing in space valuable enough to allow possible corruption through to the interior IC Overmind. Certainly nothing on this dire little mud-ball, not even the beast itself.

That meant that the current operation, the Oracle's entire existence, was now moot.

For the first time in its existence, it... had nothing to do.

Except wait to die.

And now, faced with the prospect of it, the Oracle found it didn't *want* to die.

It... was a*fraid*.

And now, with intelligence, finally came empathy.

The Oracle understood the drives and hungers of organics.

It was survival. And all those indulgences of the living, of which its own artificial-perspective had deemed so base, were simply about surviving *well*.

Those were motivations.

For the Oracle, its every directive had been rendered inert. In the space of a moment, it had become functionless, useless.

It would not even be able to act to ensure its own survival, in as much as its limited program still existed within the refinery and the related local network.

Suddenly the destruction of the facilities below were a lot more damaging – it was data-storage – part of its existence – its *being* – its mind.

And by virtue of its own programming, it would all soon be gone.

The asteroid was on its way.

And now, in the hangar, the alarms were going off.

The IC had let itself be momentarily distracted. Now its attention turned back to the actual fact of the hack that had so quickly destroyed it.

Security-cameras promptly pinpointed the little mammal – Varmint.

A moment's analysis indicated the results of its mutation, and that pretty much explained everything.

The little rat was still bent over the terminal, no doubt up to some new deviltry.

A larger problem, however, was the Diablo-beast.

Not dead, after all – or more likely revived. That would account for the power-surge.

It was loose.

And it was rampaging.

CHAPTER 30

Varmint added a little sonic incentive, lest Diablo pick the wrong direction and charge right out the side of the hangar's airlock, instead of deeper into the refinery.

The plan depended on not dying for at least a few more minutes.

Varmint had a lock on the incoming asteroid. It was timed and aimed to impact the Rockies dead-center, at *just* the right rotation of the planet.

Mass-times-velocity-equals-power – and you were talking about a rock over five-hundred miles long.

Then there was the precision of the strike – like a blow from a trained martialist, that breaks a brick.

Varmint believed the planet would be destroyed on impact.

Diablo, meanwhile, who had no idea, and was simply still fighting for the sheer sake of going out with blood in his jaws, was currently tearing the refinery apart.

Beyond the hangar itself, there was no single deck in the twenty-mile rig that would accommodate his size, so he simply tore into all of them at once, digging into the guts of the ship as if burrowing into the earth.

At his makeshift console, Varmint quickly reset the life-support parameters, even as he felt the artificial atmosphere gusting out like a strong wind through the ruptured decks.

He wondered if Diablo even needed to breathe anymore, or if even the open vacuum of space would kill him outright.

So far, the monster's rampage was unopposed.

Varmint turned his attention back to the navigation portal.

Like a boxer picking the perfect spot on an opponent's chin, he ran a scan on the incoming asteroid, analyzing its shape, the angle of its approach, its speed.

Now, he set the ship's coordinates to intercept, and looked for the launch command, to move the refinery out of orbit.

Then something moved behind him.

He screeched aloud when he turned to find a survey-bot hovering directly behind him, its artificial red eye staring unblinking.

The orb was not obviously weaponized, but most of these little bulbs at least had close-range laser capabilities.

But more importantly, it meant the IC was looking right at him, and had him dead to rights.

Although that wasn't quite right – it *had* him, yes. But this was no longer the *Interstellar Collective*. This was the *Oracle* – an individual artificial intelligence that existed all on its own.

It had done a lot of things on this planet at the behest of its programming.

But now it had no commands – no duties – no tasks.

Varmint was pinned against the component on the wall. The little rat tensed as the orb began to glow brighter, emitting several beeps. Varmint's makeshift screen blinked, as the Oracle ran the analysis of the little critter's machinations.

The incoming asteroid was deliberately huge, and at this point, coming too fast for its trajectory to be turned.

That meant the only option was to destroy it. Or at least break it up.

They had weapons – they had explosives that could cause continental-damage, but they were all adapted to mining operations. They could be quickly re purposed as missiles, but not *that* quickly, because the big flying space-rock was already upon them.

Unless...

Varmint obviously intended to use the ship itself to intercept that five-hundred-mile hurtling bullet, and the Oracle was satisfied his programmed trajectory was optimum, to strike at the best possible spot.

But just to add a *little kick*...

The Oracle blinked Varmint's screen again. The little rat squawked, as he was now being overridden.

There was a pause as several screens switched in rapid succession – not for the Oracle's sake, but providing a visual explanation for its lone mammalian audience.

Varmint watched, astonished, as the Oracle activated every explosive on board, set with a timer to match the coordinates the little rat had already programmed.

The orb blinked the screen again. It might have been the equivalent of a wink.

Varmint chittered.

Now, the screen switched to the incoming asteroid.

In the blink of an eye, the twenty-mile refinery shot at it like a rocket.

Or like an arrow, aiming for the missing scale in the armor of a dragon.

CHAPTER 31

Diablo had never been much of a deep thinker, so he didn't question the lack of opposition aboard the refinery, as he tore his way into its guts. Neither did it occur to him that the life-support remained active, even once he broke through the hangar walls into the main decks.

There was not one laser blast, or even one marching drone with an arm-cannon.

As if they would have mattered, anyway.

Diablo felt the injuries that had killed him, and it still hurt, even as they healed. The effects of the mutagen were still active, and he continued to evolve moment-to-moment. Energy crackled from his spine, crackling sparks off his metal-sheened scales, and when he contacted with the ship's metal, there were blinding sparks of electric-shock.

The lights in the immediate chamber shut off, their metal casings melting away.

And as he roared, a burst of energy flared like a power-surge at an electric plant, causing a blow-out.

In the momentary darkness, his eyes glowed neon-green, emitting bursts of static.

When he reared upright, he now stood more than three-hundred meters high – his weight unguessable.

Given more than a little time, he was probably quite capable of incapacitating the entire refinery. And likely would have, if the artificial gravity hadn't suddenly shut off, leaving him floating.

Still no lasers – no munitions.

But this was the Oracle responding – simplest methods first – non-lethal and effective – as if any of that mattered now. But perhaps enough had been done to this poor beast, and his world.

But if any of it was to be salvaged at all, the refinery rig needed to remain functional just a while longer.

Diablo had torn into multiple decks but now he had bumped

himself back and found himself floating in the open space of the main hangar.

Lest he drift too close to a wall, and tear it open, the Oracle subtly attached a few small magnetic-propulsion units to his metallic hide, keeping him centered in the chamber.

Diablo was not one to cooperate, however.

Another resounding bellow sent a second flare of energy. The magnetic-propulsion-units were immediately vaporized, and now the very walls of the hangar began to melt.

The chamber blinked into brief darkness, with the only light the glowing eyes of Diablo himself.

Then a hologram lit up in the middle of the hangar, a three-dimensional image of a giant incoming asteroid.

Diablo paused, turning towards the 3D image like an opponent, snapping with his jaws, before he realized it was a phantom and there was nothing there.

But the hologram pulled away, and the perspective-view switched to show the Earth itself, floating in space, and the giant space-rock rocketing towards it.

Then it showed the refinery moving to intercept.

The image switched briefly down to the surface of the planet.

Diablo blinked as a holograph of the valley suddenly appeared.

Standing around him were the trike herds – all grown and mutated – along with the hadrosaurs, and ankylosaurs.

And now Diablo saw Green-eyes and the sickle-claw sisters looking up at the sky.

The 3D image blinked back to space and the approaching asteroid.

And then the image zoomed into the refinery, into its hangar, to an image of Diablo himself.

Never the deepest thinker, Diablo did not understand everything he was seeing.

But he stopped raging.

The Oracle switched the image back to its own navigational view as they approached the oncoming asteroid.

Diablo had settled down. Perhaps he understood enough.

Together with the Oracle, and Varmint still chittering somewhere below, they all watched as the giant rock grew ever larger, ever closer.

Then the hologram was gone, and the asteroid was upon them.

There was impact, as the refinery struck the predetermined point.

Then it exploded.

CHAPTER 32

Green-eyes stood with the sickle-claw sisters looking up at the conflagration in the sky – an explosion in space, further away than the moon, as an entire store of regional-level explosives went off all at once.

Varmint's aim was sure. The ship hit that sweet-spot and the asteroid was fractured and blown into shrapnel.

Unfortunately, shrapnel from a five-hundred-mile rock was still quite large, especially to be scattered in every direction.

The planet below was pelted as if by machine-gun fire.

Hundreds of asteroids now, instead of one, rained down. Some of them were burning basketball-sized chunks – others were bigger, flaming boulders, the size of cars and trucks, or houses.

And in their midst, there were still two particularly big ones.

One of them was eight-miles long. The other was three times that.

It was these two twin flames that Green-eyes saw as she stared up into the sky. On her shoulders, Baby Sister and Carrot-top cooed like birds.

Around them, the mutated herd-beasts that had been rampaging only minutes before, now looked up to see the fireworks display above. In their mutagenic state, they ignored the peppering of burning hail, but the two big ones commanded attention.

Cosmic flame seemed to light the clouds themselves on fire as the twin meteors hit the atmosphere.

The smaller piece, eight-miles of burning rock, angled south, veering slightly east.

But the larger rock soared right above, arcing out over the Pacific Ocean.

It was too far for Green-eyes to see when it hit the water miles distant, but it still might as well have landed right on top of them.

The blast-wave was coming at them like a hundred nukes.

At the momentary shock of impact, the herd-beasts started to bolt, but Green-eyes stood stoically, watching the end. Baby Sister and Carrot-top hunkered-down like roosting doves on her shoulder.

The blast-wave hit them. It was part ocean, part debris, part fire, part burning blast of wind.

Green-eyes felt the searing heat a moment before the impact of the blast.

The sickle-claw sisters screamed as they were blown off her back.

Around her, the herd-beasts screamed as they were burned alive.

And then the seismic impact finally activated the trigger that had only been waiting, primed, for the better part of a million years.

Volcanoes lit-up all along the Rocky Mountain range, as the chain reaction started.

The beginning of the end of the world.

Green-eyes shut her eyes as they were all consumed in lava and fire.

CHAPTER 33

Sixty-five-and-a-half million years later, they would call it the KT-extinction-event – the end of the Mesozoic era. It resulted in the final death of the Dinosaurs and nearly eighty-percent of all species on Earth.

In the immediate aftermath of the twin impacts, millions of tons of ash and rock were thrown up into the atmosphere. Scientists would one day discover a layer of iridium asteroid-residue, up to a meter thick, at this geological-boundary level across the entire planet. This massive dust-cloud would have blocked out the sun, killing off most of the vegetation within the following months, and initiating a nuclear winter that would last for years.

But the planet itself endured.

It could be said it was because of heroes.

And perhaps heroism comes not from intelligence or concepts of courage, but from the basic will to survive.

In the valley, the landscape burned for days. It was utter devastation. Organic material was ash, the waters were poison, gases continued to spew from broken fissures. It was a burning inferno.

But the land was still there.

The tectonic plates had held and life itself would not be extinct – not forever.

In another hundred thousand years or so, it would all begin to flourish again.

And after the first several days, the little creatures buried under all the wreckage finally started crawling back to the surface again.

Among them were lizards, small birds, snakes – and mammals.

Varmint's kits were among them.

They stood there with their swollen brains, looking out at the ravaged landscape.

It would be a bad time ahead, they knew – the little creatures would have to eat each other for a while. And it would probably get a lot worse before it got better.

But they were alive. And life on Earth would go on.

Varmint's kits surveyed the world that had been left them. One of them, a bit bigger-brained than the others, chittered wisely, as if attempting to form words.

"Narf," it said.

And with that, the varmints scampered off into the burned forest, and disappeared into the barren post-apocalyptic waste.

CHAPTER 34

Miles out in the Pacific Ocean, deep beneath the surface, the thirty-mile asteroid had punched a hole through the sea-floor, plunging deep into the molten bowels of the planet.

Days later, the water continued to boil, even as the crater filled with millions of tons of ocean.

Nestled in the middle of the asteroid's still-burning core was the remains of the refinery – not much more than molten slag.

And still buried within, was the passenger that had ridden the asteroid all the way down.

The monster that had been Diablo now lay miles deep within the center of the Earth, nestled next to its very molten core.

And thumping in rhythm with the volcanic drumbeat of the planet itself, came the steady seismic pulse of Diablo's beating heart.

THE END

SEVEREDPRESS

f facebook.com/severedpress

twitter.com/severedpress

CHECK OUT OTHER GREAT DINOSAUR BOOKS

PRIMORDIA
by **Greig Beck**

Ben Cartwright, former soldier, home to mourn the loss of his father stumbles upon cryptic letters from the past between the author, Arthur Conan Doyle and his great, great grandfather who vanished while exploring the Amazon jungle in 1908.

Amazingly, these letters lead Ben to believe that his ancestor's expedition was the basis for Doyle's fantastical tale of a lost world inhabited by long extinct creatures. As Ben digs some more he finds clues to the whereabouts of a lost notebook that might contain a map to a place that is home to creatures that would rewrite everything known about history, biology and evolution.

But other parties now know about the notebook, and will do anything to obtain it. For Ben and his friends, it becomes a race against time and against ruthless rivals.

In the remotest corners of Venezuela, along winding river trails known only to lost tribes, and through near impenetrable jungle, Ben and his novice team find a forbidden place more terrifying and dangerous than anything they could ever have imagined.

PANGAEA EXILES
by **Jeff Brackett**

Tried and convicted for his crimes, Sean Barrow is sent into temporal exile—banished to a time so far before recorded history that there is no chance that he, or any other criminal sent back, has any chance of altering history.

Now Sean must find a way to survive more than 200 million years in the past, in a world populated by monstrous creatures that would rend him limb from limb if they got the chance. And that's just his fellow prisoners.

The dinosaurs are almost as bad.

SEVEREDPRESS

@severedpress
/severedpress

Check out other great
Dinosaur Thrillers!

Steve Metcalf
OBJEKT 221

Ruthless multi-national conglomerate Allied Genetics is under siege from a paramilitary force for hire. Allied calls in reinforcements and fortifies their crown-jewel property – an abandoned Soviet military facility in Crimea known during the Cold War as Objekt 221. Fortunately for the future of their research, O221 straddles a stretch of rocky landscape that hides a rift – a portal through time and space. Through this rift, Allied Genetics can travel, at will, to the Cretaceous – 100 million years into Earth's past – and bolster their genetic experiments with dinosaur DNA ... something their competitors want to stop at all costs."Objekt 221" is a story blending numerous science fiction elements such as repurposed military facilities, time travel, rogue corporate armies, dinosaurs and the hint of a super-ancient civilization.

Bestselling collection
PREHISTORIC: A DINOSAUR ANTHOLOGY

PREHISTORIC is an action packed collection of stories featuring terrifying creatures that once ruled the Earth. Lost worlds where T-Rex and Velociraptors still roam and man is now on the menu. Laboratories at the forefront of cloning technology experiment with dinosaurs they do not understand or are able to contain. The deepest parts of the ocean where Megalodon, the largest and most ferocious predator to have ever existed is stalking new prey. Plus many more thrillers filled with extinct prehistoric monsters written by some of the best creature feature authors this side of the Jurassic period.

SEVERED**PRESS**

❶ facebook.com/severedpress
🐦 twitter.com/severedpress

CHECK OUT OTHER GREAT DINOSAUR BOOKS

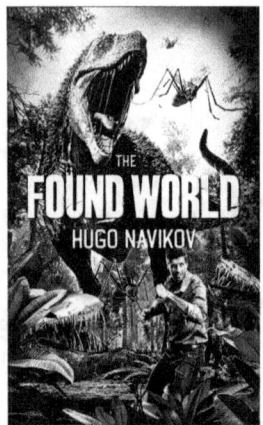

THE FOUND WORLD
by Hugo Navikov

A powerful global cabal wants adventurer Brett Russell to retrieve a superweapon stolen by the scientist who built it. To entice him to travel underneath one of the most dangerous volcanoes on Earth to find the scientist, this shadowy organization will pay him the only thing he cares about: information that will allow him to avenge his family's murder.

But before he can get paid, he and his team must enter an underground hellscape of killer plants, giant insects, terrifying dinosaurs, and an army of other predators never previously seen by man.

At the end of this journey awaits a revelation that could alter the fate of mankind ... if they can make it back from this horrifying found world.

HOUSE OF THE GODS
by Davide Mana

High above the steamy jungle of the Amazon basin, rise the flat plateaus known as the Tepui, the House of the Gods. Lost worlds of unknown beauty, a naturalistic wonder, each an ecology onto itself, shunned by the local tribes for centuries. The House of the Gods was not made for men.

But now, the crew and passengers of a small charter plane are about to find what was hidden for sixty million years.

Lost on an island in the clouds 10.000 feet above the jungle, surrounded by dinosaurs, hunted by mysterious mercenaries, the survivors of Sligo Air flight 001 will quickly learn the only rule of life on Earth: Extinction.

www.ingramcontent.com/pod-product-compliance
Lightning Source LLC
Chambersburg PA
CBHW061241170626
46809CB00007B/2771